Fall

Edited by

Katherine Anderson

Amanda Andrews

Melanie Czerwinski

DARK INK PRESS

FALL

FICTION ANTHOLOGY

EDITED BY

KATHERINE ANDERSON

AMANDA ANDREWS

MELANIE CZERWINSKI

Table of Contents

A French Too Deep for Daisies

When the USS Black Arrow made berth at New York City,
Arthur Frederick Tierney contemplated the enigma of change. Before the
war, he had glided through a monochrome of farmland and seed, cattle
and feed. The threat of drought was followed too closely by the threat of
an early freeze. Then, overnight, he became a soldier, and the threat of
death was followed too closely by the threat of trench foot, trench fever,
trench mouth. The other troops aboard the converted freighter spoke of
their homes, their families, their lives—but, even after crossing the
Atlantic, Tierney could not escape an unfilled French grave. Change
progressed linearly, with shifts to better and to worse—but always
forward, never back. Tierney's change was stalled.

He dawdled on his trip home, hopping off at depots on whims
because he caught a whiff of baking bread nearby or because measures of
"The Boys Who Won't Come Home" drifted up between the huff and
screech of the train as a town band practiced in the square. In
Pennsylvania, he followed the young woman sitting in front of him
because he'd never seen a shade of blue like that of her coat. If the cold
sting of peppermint had a color, Tierney knew it would be that blue.

The woman walked three blocks from the station and entered a
corner shoe store. Tierney watched through the front window as she
unbuttoned and hung up her coat. Over the next hour, she fitted four
people for shoes, sold pairs to three, and, putting her coat back on,
stepped outside for a break. Tierney nodded to her as she struck a match
on the shop's stone facing and lit a cigarette. He lingered just long

1

enough to check for a hint of peppermint and, finding none, walked back to the train station.

He chose his next stop because the ticket price was lucky or because he liked the name of the town; West Virginia had some of the best: Pie, Paw Paw, Big Ugly. Once in Ohio, Tierney bought a ticket, stood on the boarding platform, and just watched the engine steam away.

The day Tierney's money ran out, he rode the L&N line to Resverie, a backwoods Kentucky town. The people moved slower there, as if they'd spent all their energy that winter stretching up from the valley, yearning for the hidden sun that peeped between the lanky trees of Black Mountain's slopes. Now that spring had begun to thaw the creeks and loamy soil, people eased their gaze downward to the muddy pathways. Tierney compromised as he wandered the streets, looking straight ahead at the weathered whitewash of fences and siding, at the crooked lines of buildings that strove for a true vertical but, lacking a precedent, shared the list and pitch of the yellow poplars and hickories.

Battered leftover propaganda nailed crookedly to a post caught Tierney's eye. The paper was inching its way off the nails, tearing more with each flutter. **STAND BY THE BOYS IN THE TRENCHES. MINE MORE COAL**, the US Fuel Administration ordered. The miner and his pickaxe stood back-to-back with the soldier and his rifle—vigilant, serious, dry—backlit by a glorious blaze of yellow-orange light. Tierney knew the artist had never been in a trench, and he doubted a mine either. A final breeze caught the poster and ripped it free. It wrapped around the spoke of a wagon wheel for a moment and then was gone.

Tierney's gaze was drawn to the front of the wagon where two men were working to replace the left wheel. As one of the men hefted the box, Tierney saw him through a haze of gunfire and smoke, hearing the whiz and whir of bullets overhead near Château-Thierry. The Germans had been close enough that lead wouldn't be the primary threat within a few minutes. Instead, they'd be up against saw-bladed bayonets and trench knives. *Seitengewehr* and *Nahkampfmesser*, the translator said they were called, in a language as fierce and harsh as the weapons themselves. The combat cart, waylaid by a broken axle and stubborn mule, had only just arrived. But John Tate hefted a Hotchkiss without a mount and—loosing a shrill, jolting yell not sounded with such soul since before Appomattox—started firing. Tierney scrambled to keep the machine gun fed with the 30-round strips. John's actions saved them all that day—not for the last time either.

Standing in the middle of the street in Resverie, Tierney stared ahead, fighting the urge to lift his hands to his ears against the evoked bedlam. The other man spun the repaired wagon wheel on the axle, tightened the nut, and John eased down the box. As he turned to shake the other man's hand, John caught sight of Tierney, returning his stare with a wave of a ham of a hand, tentatively as if John, too, might have been peering through a haze of memory.

The other man turned to hitch a team to the wagon, and John, slinging a bulging burlap bag over his shoulder, started toward Tierney. John moved with the easy, limber stroll of the athletic and the strong. One of his hands would have done fine to envelop Tierney's, but he used two, gripping with such fervor that Tierney finally believed his friend was corporeal.

"Butter my butt an' call me a biscuit!" John roared. "I says to myself, 'that can't be Aft! It just can't!' But land sakes alive, sure as I'm standin' here, here you are!"

3

John finally released his grip, and Tierney relaxed at the familiar nickname. It had started off badly with a commanding officer commenting that Tierney was always behind, always last, and taking every opportunity to imply cowardice as to the reason Tierney's initials fit so well. But as soon as John declared Aft was behind because he had their backs and always would, even the officer shut his mouth. The name took on an endearment, and no one, safe Tierney himself, questioned his cowardice again.

"What are you doin' in Resverie? You're a long way from home."

Tierney hesitated. John's warmth and strength seemed unchanged. Tierney felt like a scuffling shadow. "Thought I'd do some sightseeing on my way," Tierney offered. "Why aren't you in New Orleans with your girl?" She must have written John three times a week, and Tierney had pictured the couples' lives together in letter after letter. When the mail dispatch arrived, sometimes John would have eight or nine piled up in delivery. The squad lived on John's letters.

Gorilla mitts, as John called them, were not well-suited for writing. He said his script was "messier'n a coonhound and a porcupine sharin' a beehive." He asked Tierney to write as he spoke, and Tierney obliged. Tierney spent many hours squinting at the paper by French moonlight. He figured it was as close as he'd ever come to poetry.

John's wide brow crinkled like a linen handkerchief, and his tongue made a full, slow circuit, bulging out the skin around his lips. He had the most expressive face Tierney had ever seen and the personality to match.

"Got a letter in Saint-Nazaire before I left France. She's married now."

Tierney felt the blow himself. Miss Vistoire Volant of 724 Dumaine Street, New Orleans, Louisiana, hadn't just been John's love. She and her lavender-scented letters belonged to all of them, though none would have said it.

"Her mama never thought I was near good 'nuf, you recall. She found Vistoire a—what did she term it—a *sooot-able* match." John shrugged. "For the best, I suppose. Mama had another babe an' took sick to her bed after I left before the war, and them with the five girls already. Mama met her maker six months ago, an' Pa owes the company store." John looked down to his booted feet and cleared his throat. "There's debts to be paid, Aft. I shouldn'ta never gone away before the war."

The two men spoke a bit about their trips back to the states. John had been among some of the first to arrive back on a commandeered German vessel. Tierney had crossed the Atlantic a couple months later.

"Why don't you come on home? I'm sure Sissy's 'bout done cookin' supper."

Tierney nodded, and John clapped him on the back. As they approached a row of whitewashed shacks, John's face darkened, and he spit in the dirt. "We had a cabin some seven miles yonder," he tossed an arc up the western mountainside with his hand, "but when I was away, Pa moved the family to the coal company's housing. Our cabin wasn't much finer 'n this, but if I'd of stayed . . ." His voice faded away as three rail-thin girls in rags piled out the door of the third shack on the left.

"John!" They shouted his name as they scurried toward him. He tossed the littlest onto his shoulder and the other two clutched at his canvas trousers, all talking a mile a minute with accents so thick Tierney only caught scraps about a sick cat and a skinned possum and something called a dying duck fit.

They climbed the rickety steps into the house, and Tierney met the rest of John's family: two girls around thirteen or fourteen taking turns stirring the watery contents of a steaming pot on the stove, a toddler beating a stick against the wall with intermittent screeches, and their father swaying in a rough-hewn rocking chair, tapping a harmonica on his knee in rhythm with the toddler's stick. The man's sunken eyes and shadowed cheeks reminded Tierney of a bleached skull. He wondered as he shook the man's hand how a vigorous titan such as John had come from him.

"Welcome, son. We can't give you much, but we give you what we got left." John's father spoke in a dry rasp that rose and fell, and Tierney thought he heard a quiet echo of a giant.

After a bowl of radish and possum stew, Tierney sat outside with John and smoked a cigarette. "Mama'n'em would say there's rain comin'," John said, motioning to the bleary ring around the bright moon. Then he glanced toward the house and spoke in a low rumble. "If I had my druthers, I'd of gone to New Orleans even if Vistoire didn't want me. The land's so low even their dead is above ground."

Tierney nodded and blew a haze of smoke over the moon. "Maybe if she saw you, she'd remember—"

John chuckled. "She'd remember alright. Don't ken how she forgot in the first place. I reckon her mama just wore her down." He lit his own cigarette and exhaled with a cough. "Happens to folks. Pa—he's jest wore slap out. He can't go down in the mine no more, an' like I says, there's debts to be paid." John squirmed and fiddled with his cigarette, and Tierney recognized the gesture as John's preamble to a confession. "I never—I never had a lick of trouble before the war, Aft. But now . . . hell, the pit in my stomach's done deeper'n that hole in the ground. Some days I jest freeze up. The foreman—" He gave a scoffing snicker followed by another cough. "The foreman called me 'a good-for-nothin' git.' I ain't . . . I *always* been good for somethin'."

Relaxing into the companionship of shadows, Tierney thought about the poster in town, the coal miner and the doughboy standing back-to-back. "Takes time, I suppose," he said. John nodded.

Tierney considered the nerves involved to take up a pickaxe and descend hundreds of feet into a hole in the ground by lamplight. Then he thought of his own debts to be paid. They didn't even suit the same balance.

Tierney cleared his throat. "I'm looking for some work. Ran out of money for the trip home. What do you have to do to get hired on?" Tierney saw John's gratitude in his eyes but chose to attribute their watery look to the strange glow from the ring around the moon.

The next morning at first light, Tierney was outfitted with a pickaxe, a carbide lamp with extra carbide, water, and matches, and a cloth cap with a leather brim and bracket for the lamp. He was told the company would take the cost for the gear out of his first pay.

Tierney fought to keep the march from his step. With heads held high, led by John's easy smile, and without a scuffling shadow in sight, they crowded into the cage and were lowered down the mine shaft. When a timber cracked two hours later, no one smiled. Tierney was shoved hard in the scramble of racing men in a shower of earth, and his head bounced off the rocky wall face.

Arthur Frederick Tierney opened his eyes at the bottom of the coal mine just shy of Resverie. His face and side were pressed against the cold wall where he had fallen. He turned his head feebly with searing pain. The grainy outline of John's body next to him was just visible in the dim light of a dying lamp. His great chest heaved once. Twice. "Them debts ain't got no mercy." John's words were a blind whisper, floating on his finished breath, and change shed its enigma.

Mattie Lee Monroe

Big Blue World

"Where did the idea come from?"

Despite their best efforts, there was a fly in the room, and it was tracing slow, lazy circles against the featureless white ceiling. The painter's attention was fixating on it; he was ignoring the question.

" The painting. Your most recent painting, where did the idea come from?" Her voice was patient, gentle. She'd even used his stupid moniker. They had said it would make him more likely to cooperate.

He licked his lips. There was an unhealthy sheen about him, something sticky and unpleasant to the texture of his skin. His eyes were bloodshot and fever-bright.

"Wasn't no idea, was there? Wasn't no idea," he muttered. He'd dropped his carefully constructed artiste vocabulary sometime last week, after they took away his painting. Now he was flat, sapless, ordinary.

She hated the interrogations. She'd always hated the interrogations.

"Do you remember if there was a particular event that inspired you to paint *A Study In Blue*?" The words were carefully chosen. She knew exactly what had inspired the man's sprawled, intricate canvas, but she needed to know where he had seen it, and who else might have seen it when he did. They were getting there; they were climbing the ladder. This guy was close to the source.

He shifted. Licked his lips again. Sucked in a hitched breath.

"Don't matter, does it?" He was angry suddenly. "Don't matter, you won't even let me finish it. You won't even—"

Silence. The fly was banging against the two-way mirror, its fleshy little body thumping against the glass. He was shivering, his fingers bending at sharp angles. They always got this way if interrupted—near the end all they wanted to do was get it done, get it made, share their magnum opus with the world. It became their reason to live.

"We'll let you finish it," she promised quietly. She was speaking slowly, as if to a child. "We'll let you finish and share it if you can tell us where the idea came from to paint it."

He tensed. There was a pathetic glimmer of hope in his eyes—if he wasn't this far gone, he wouldn't have bought the lie, but she had him.

"Berlin. Babylon. The gate." He licked his lips again. "Can I go now? Can I have it back and go now? I—"

But she was already moving, chair scraping across the floor. The click of heels was followed by the click of the lock. The solitary fly buzzed frantically against the window, little legs scraping the glass.

They'd laughed when she told them. It had been a suicide case, at first, and then a spate of suicide cases linked by a crucial factor, and then a hunt for a potential serial killer with an exotic modus operandi.

"You're saying the colour is killing them?" He was grinning, but the look in his eyes was closer to disbelief than amusement. "That's ridiculous, Fee."

"You're thinking about it wrong," she'd said, shaking her head. She was on the tail end of another all-nighter. "Look at what we've got to work with, all right? Look at the pattern. All of these people were artists of some kind—painters or designers, even a bloody tailor. All of them made something big, something impressive, and then killed themselves. And the thing they make is always blue, right? It's always that same goddamned shade of blue."

Her boss was shaking his head. "We've been through this. It's a killer who contacts them, blackmails them into—"

"With what? With what, Nolan? We've found no evidence of blackmail anywhere, and it's a—" she glanced to the desk, pulling files from the fraying binder, laying them out. "He," she said, tapping a photo, "went to *her* opening. Then *this* one bought the dress he made a few days later. Then this guy found *her* painting, don't you see it's a pattern? It's not just one person at a time, it propagates, it's—" She stopped suddenly, searching for words. Her fingers were tight against the wood of the desk. "Don't think of it as a colour, think of it as a madness, or a-a virus. It infects, then it gestates, then it spreads." Her voice was shaky. "I've spoken to some psychologists, neurobiologists. They say—"

He wouldn't listen. He put her on stress leave at first, until he found his daughter in her studio with a note and the wrong colour up to her elbows. He didn't understand. He said he'd been fine. He'd just shown her the artwork; she just wanted to see, but it only ever took the artists, the people who really saw the colour. What she'd made was beautiful. It was the first piece locked up as evidence, in an opaque plastic crate. Weeks later they were piled high.

It became impossible to keep quiet from then on. The word spread like wildfire—incredulous messages popped up in social media and scientific journals, witty critiques filled reputable newspapers and news anchors repeated phrases like, "Is the government really spending taxpayer dollars to censor a colour?"

They didn't know which colour, of course. Every piece of artwork connected to the case had been confiscated as evidence, and when they became inaccessible, the torrent of deaths quickly slowed to a trickle.

She met Martin during the media firestorm, one of the only sympathetic faces from the other side. He was a footage editor for one of the big names. After working on a prime time special casting her in the light of a lunatic inspector, he sent her an apologetic email. He believed her, he said, he'd seen it happen to his brother. They met for an interview over coffee. He was quiet and focused, and almost a better help to her than her own team was. When they finished, he asked her if she wanted to go out for coffee again sometime.

He came to the station when they were discussing the cryptic admission by Mr. Indigo, and he lingered. It was his case too in a way, and he knew what the painter had meant.

"The Ishtar gates of Babylon—they're in the Pergamon museum, Berlin." His teeth were slightly crooked; you could see it when he spoke, just poking out from the upper lip. She'd grown to find it endearing somehow.

"Oh, I've seen those!" The new intern, Emma, was a bubbly sort. "But a lot of people have. Wouldn't there be more deaths than there are? If they're the wrong blue—that blue—then they're all over the internet, too."

Martin frowned and sipped from his chipped mug, a novelty piece from a forgotten film.

She was right: there were too many people to trace, to find, and if everyone had spread the colour... but there would have been more deaths, surely? It would be common knowledge, a phenomenon, not contained like this. Fee opened the Wikipedia page on the Ishtar gate, scrolling down and skimming until the clicking of the little wheel in the mouse became a tense whirr.

"There are two. One's in the Pergamon archives. Is there a chance he saw that one?" She stood. Emma started typing. "I'll check it out. You two will be late."

At the restaurant, the waiter recognised her and someone had laughed. They went to a drive-by instead and ate in the car. She didn't mind; her job was her life now, that was all. There was no sense fighting it.

"There might be a list of people the curators let into the museum archives to see the gate. Or they might remember." Martin was watching her thoughtfully as he talked, wiping greasy fingers on a paper napkin. It was a good idea. Progress, even hypothetical progress, made the sting of the mockery burn a little less.

He came home with her that night, and the company was nice. He found her with a laptop in the early morning sending off emails in clumsy German, and she told him she'd slept well for the first time in months. He smiled with his lips closed. He did that when he didn't want people to see his teeth.

She wasn't sure why she lied; she knew he wouldn't have minded the truth, but she wanted him to feel like he was special, more than just an interlude in the flat, hungry dreams of a world as blue and empty as the sky above it.

Martin was right: they did remember, and a list was made soon after. It was extensive. Identity checks were done on every name, and every artist singled out and contacted. Pieces were confiscated, each one the start of its own breadcrumb trail, its own domino chain reaction of lethal artwork and feverish obsession. Each name lead to others, every artist releasing their lethal magnum opus, blossoming the same chromatic madness into all those that saw it.

They started to make probable lists, too; next of kin with an artistic bent, or clients with notable hobbies... the task was impossible. Containing it, all of it, would never be done. But they could weather the storm, fight the plague. Some of the artists could even be saved with amnesiacs; the freshly exposed, or the faintly colourblind. Others were too far gone for even extreme memory loss to help, remembering nothing other than the intensity, wasting away from the subconscious obsession alone.

The months blurred together. They had the source now, though no specialist could explain what it was about Babylon's blue-glazed bricks that started the madness. The deaths were slowing to one reported every few months. International law enforcement had the green light to join them, and very quickly she was knocked down from leader of the operation to one of innumerable field agents. She didn't mind; it didn't matter who was spearheading it. It just had to work.

There were accidents. Broadening the scope of it meant bringing more people in, and some of those people had a creative bent that had escaped the screening. They all quickly learned to recognise the signs in their colleagues— the feverishness, the fascination with details, the unhealthy obsession with their One Great Work, whatever it may be, and the inevitable end. Emma had been hired for a while—she was an amateur writer, she'd said, but they had assumed a colourless hobby was safe.

It wasn't.

"It needs a name," she'd said. "We can't keep calling it 'that' blue or 'the wrong colour'. It needs a proper name."

None of her names were ever quite right. She went through eight, tweaking them all minorly, and grew increasingly irritable with anyone calling it anything she'd decided was inadequate. They didn't think much of it; everyone was high-strung. Everyone was under pressure. Then one day she didn't turn up at all. She'd synthesised the shade into hex code, under which she pinned a shakily written note with the final name she settled on: Babylon Blue.

Fee took it in stride, but it hit Martin hard, and he was angry at how little she was ruffled. It was like she hadn't even blinked, he said. He was wrong, but she wasn't sure how to tell him, wasn't sure what it meant that the thing that was haunting her the most was that six-figure code. A few weeks later, the legislation passed confirming "B-Blue" as a legally valid cause of death in seven countries. Social media trends quickly started calling it "Big

Blue," a thing spoken of in hushed tones when serious and brazen ones were joking.

The confiscated artworks had to be moved to a series of warehouses at first, and then when the warehouses were piled full, they had to be destroyed. There was no point storing ornamentals that couldn't be sold and couldn't be appreciated. Martin said it was a shame. Fee snuck him in to show him the most impressive ones, the most intricate. She made him wear tinted swimming goggles. "It's an art," she said flatly. "What you do. Can't take the risk."

She showed him the first—her favourite still: a stained glass Tiffany lamp with a motif of B-blue flowers. It had been damaged in transit, and an edge was jagged and warped. He'd fretted more about the cut than she did. Then she showed him the original fragments of the gate, the age old ceramics. A forensics team had combed the place and chipped out those parts that corresponded exactly with the spectrum of B-blue, neutralising the source. There was very little of it, only enough to fill an underwhelming cup. She showed him the paintings, so many bloody paintings, every one of them anguished and sincere and beautiful. This is the swan song people make, she told him. This is what happens when you burn your life up making a thing.

They sat outside the dump when the incineration started, sipping coffee from a thermos flask, his fingers curled through hers. The smoke that drifted up from the furnaces was reassuringly gray, as colourless as anything could be. Martin was chewing his lip.

"I still think they should have been kept somewhere." He saw significance in them only because people had died, she realised.

"They're too dangerous. After tonight there won't be anything left. No one else can get sick, infected, whatever it is." She sipped from the flask, and passed it back to him. "Besides. One of them was a chef. He made B-blue sauce. I don't know how we're supposed to store that for posterity." She tried a smile.

He winced. "Don't joke about this," he muttered. "Please." There was a pause, and a sip, and the flask came back to her. When she brushed against them his fingers were cold. "Want to sleep at my place tonight?" It was a murmur, not amorous, though he was trying to make it sound that way. He just wanted to know she wouldn't be sleeping at the station again.

"I can't. We're almost done. Another few weeks; there are only a few names left, and then it's over, Martin. I promise you. It'll be over."

"Okay," he said, finishing the coffee. He drove Fee back to work.

The worst one took them by surprise. Alice Rollins wasn't on their list. They had been reaching the end of it, fighting the exponential fractal, and then one of the tracking algorithms picked her up—a high-caliber architect with erratic behaviour. She was buying paint by the barrel, returning it days later with demands for a refund. They found increasingly agitated emails—not the right colour, I was very specific, it's not bright enough, it's not deep enough, isn't this your job—and then nothing.

Alice Rollins became Fee's personal obsession. She had disappeared; flat empty, splattered and decaying, friends unaware or unhelpful. She'd dropped her phone, emptied her bank account, and wasn't distinctive enough to easily track.

There was something cathartic about the old fashioned chase. Fee worked on the record and off of it, spiraling out from the last sighting with the regularity of a machine; a diamond point scratching vinyl grooves of bitchumen. White noise was all she got at first, and then there was rumour, and gossip, and, finally, an address. It's always a motel. Fee had brought a gun but wouldn't need it; it had been months since exposure. Alice Rollins was too far gone to be dangerous.

The once-architect was kneeling in pools of colour, scooping and smearing pigment. It was blue, all of it, but none was *that* shade, none of it burned bright enough, cut deep enough. She couldn't recreate it. It was too elusive.

Fee had seen B-blue. She sat with Alice Rollins on the tile and painted with her fingers; adding, subtracting, amending, starting again. It was a nuance of a nuance, subtle enough to be hidden in plain sight. It was missed as a smudge in a colour wheel by millions of searching eyes until it was extrapolated, focused upon. It was deadliest when cultivated.

She found out the next day that the last name on their list had been cleared. Weeks passed, and the mood became hopeful. A month passed, and it was officially called. The infectious spread of B-blue was over. The colour remained an uncontainable threat, but it had become a latent one; a virus of which the deadly, propagating strain was now culled.

That night, Martin called to tell her a six-part documentary exposé about it was being organised, and she was being asked to consult on it, and she was going to be a hero. He invited her to the editing suite for the live announcement. "It's only fair," he'd said with a smile in his voice, "that you spend some time at my work with all the time I've spent at yours."

He was grinning and she could see his crooked teeth when he sipped from the champagne glass. It was dark and warm and the room was full of people tapping quietly away, teasing sliders, touching up freeze-frames. He was relaxed, she could tell. It had been weeks since it had been this easy to be around him. The tension was gone, the animosity was gone.

"Feels wrong I wasn't there for the last one," she said quietly between sips, "Like I missed the ending." He gave her hand a squeeze.

"You were there for the first. And you fixed this; you put the wheels into motion."

Her eyes drifted to the screen. It was still too fresh; it didn't feel like a victory. She didn't feel like a hero. "Why is it red?" She asked between sips. He quirked an eyebrow. "This thing," she clarified, tapping the screen.

"That's the banner. It's the colour for the channel. Why?" When he clicked, it became outlined in yellow, and a little edit menu filled the left of the screen.

"Live in three," came the warning through the speakers.

He grinned and slipped a hand around her. "It's over finally. And once this is out, the slate will be clean. You'll be able to get your life back."

As he was talking, she teased the mouse from his fingers, eyes going half-lidded. She wasn't listening, and he was wrapped too deeply in his relief to tell. "I don't know what I'll do," she said quietly. "This was my project. My thing. It's kept me going for so long now."

"Live in two."

Martin frowned, lazily, like someone waking from a dream, only just now sensing the tension in the air. Something was wrong—Fee's eyes were hazy, and she was clicking hungrily at the screen. He didn't mind; she wasn't changing anything, just looking at the settings, but soon—

"Live in one."

He tried to tug her hands gently away from the keyboard. "Come on, Fee, it'll be on air in a second," he said softly, but she wasn't moving. Her limbs were taut and shaking, and her skin was hot and clammy. The realisation hit him like a brick.

Fee had found the colour editor—one of those old hex code ones, a wide bowl of shades with six little spaces at the bottom. There was a dull ringing in Martin's ears, like the pitched whine that follows an explosion. "Fee," he stammered. "Fee, what are you doing? Fee—"

"We're live!"

Ben Brown

Stimulant

We stopped at a Wawa—an old Wawa with a busted roof and barely any gas pumps. Theo was hungry, and I desperately needed something to jolt me awake. My first concern was the ice and snow on the roof. The whole place looked like it could fall in on itself at any second, and if I had any say in it, I wasn't going to die getting crushed by the Wawa Icee machine.

I clutched the car door handle. "Should we really leave the car alone?"

"No one will be suspicious unless you *make* them suspicious. Come on." He gave a reassuring smile and got out first, as if setting an example for how I should act.

My shoes stuck to the dirty floors and half of the machines were out of order, but it was the best we'd get until the next rest stop another forty miles away. In the short span of time allotted while my cup filled with coffee, I wondered why I was in this exact place at this exact time. Something about the blinding artificial lights and people coming and going within minutes made it the perfect place for ridiculously philosophical thoughts to creep up. Liminal spaces and all that.

"You alright?"

Theo was cradling a blue raspberry Icee with the straw already nestled between his lips, stuffed pretzels bites, and some leftover breakfast sandwich they still had out for some reason. We already had various snacks he threw in the backseat before he picked me up, so I couldn't help but wonder how long he thought we would be on the road.

"Yeah. Yeah, I'm fine. Just tired."

I pushed the plastic lid down on my coffee with a tight snap.

"Oh, I hear that, trust me."

He'd been up all night, he told me earlier. His eyes were wide and bright, but in these lights, he had clear shadows under his eyes. I studied him for a moment, but that smile didn't leave his face. I grabbed a few of whatever sweeteners my hand landed on and nodded.

He hauled everything to the checkout and plopped it down, crossing his arms as he glanced up at the cigarettes behind the counter.

"Can I have a pack of, uh," Theo narrowed his eyes at the wide variety of tobacco. "I don't know, like, menthols?" He made a rolling motion with his index finger and thumb, simulating the crushing of a menthol capsule in the filter. The only kind he had ever had when he bummed them off friends.

The cashier grabbed a pack of Marlboros and added it to the total. Theo gave a wide smile and "thanks" after handing over his cash. I only gave a small dip of my head in acknowledgment, not taking my lips away from my cup.

I took small steps toward the car, trying to delay my inevitable arrival to the passenger door. Was the trunk weighing down the rest of the car? At Theo's urging, I quickened my pace so I could help him open the door without spilling his feast.

We settled into the old Toyota and continued back north up I-95. The interior was covered in receipts and crumbs and had the lingering scent of oily fast food, as Theo was never one for cleaning until it was a near health hazard. We'd been on the road for about three and a half hours by then, but Theo hadn't said where we were going.

I rubbed the sleep from my eyes as I turned up the heater that blasted directly into my face. Straightening up and letting my back hit the seat with a thump, I looked out the window. Blankets of snow weighed down the skeletons of trees, their dark trunks tired. The pavement was slick with melted ice and peppered with salt crystals from a truck that couldn't have passed by too long before we did. The busted left speaker made me feel like only half of my head was working. I pressed my temple to the cold glass and squeezed my eyes shut.

"You ever been on a road trip before?" Theo didn't take his eyes away from the road. I always told him I was fine with silence, but he'd always shift and hum and come up with something to say to fill the space.

"No." I reached into my bag and popped a muscle relaxer to try and ease the ache deep in my body.

"They're not so fun here. I went on one when I was in SoCal before. *That* was awesome."

I nodded and looked down at the cuff of my sweatshirt, pulling at the ribbed knit and watching it snap back into place.

"That was a good concert, huh?" He gestured toward the logo on my sweatshirt. I hadn't coined Theo as someone who liked industrial metal, but he raved about how much he loved it the entire drive home. It was about three sizes too big, but it was all they had left by the time we got to the merch table. *Get it anyway*, Theo had yelled to me over the buzz in our ears. He held his arms up with limp wrists. *It'll look cute with the sleeves really long.*

The sweatshirt was the warmest piece of clothing near my bed when his call woke me up. He sounded calm over the phone, which only made me worry that much more. It wasn't in his character to ever be calm, only upbeat to a fault. He told me he'd be at my house in forty minutes, and that I should bring a change of clothes and some food. I realized ten minutes into the drive from my house, trying not to fall asleep in my giant sweatshirt, that I hadn't even questioned it.

Theo, presumably tired from his long night, drifted off the road just far enough for the tires to drop off the asphalt and onto the dirt, the jolt sending hot coffee up my nose.

"Shit."

"I'm sorry!" He looked from the road to me and back in rapid succession, reaching out with one hand as he tried to think of how to help. I waved him off and reached for the glove compartment, assuming there would be napkins in it, only for him to grab my wrist with terrifying speed and strength.

Leaning toward the passenger seat with his left hand gripping the wheel, he drove shakily as he stared directly into my eyes. His face, void of any emotion, was a threat in itself. I didn't know it was an expression he was capable of making. He eventually let go and turned his attention back to the road when he noticed two cars passing him, the drivers probably having a fit at his shit driving. I could only gawk dumbly at his profile, coffee still dripping from my nostrils and onto my lap. At the very least, the blood flow to my hand wasn't blocked off anymore.

"There're napkins in there, just... be really careful."

With that warning, I was much more willing to snort the coffee up and deal with it than find out what the hell was in the glove compartment. That is, until it started to drip down my throat and I winced at the burn. I opened the latch with a single finger, my other hand resting on the curved underside to let it open as slowly as possible. Resting on top of brown napkins, straws, and an ancient Dunkin' Donuts gift card was a handgun.

My hands flew back on instinct, afraid that if they were anywhere near the gun it would somehow go off.

"The safety's on," he reassured me as he bit off a chunk of a stuffed pretzel.

Nodding weakly, I carefully picked up the gun to get to the napkins underneath, immediately putting it back and closing the compartment. I looked at him from the corner of my eye as I held the napkins up to my nose, but he was focused on the road. His expression had softened while I was cleaning myself up. I blew my nose and let out a disgusted sigh of relief. I used the other napkins the try and blot the coffee from my pants.

"I didn't know you even owned a gun."

"I don't. I took it from my dad."

I felt my brow furrow. "He doesn't seem like the type to own guns."

"Well, he took it from Granddad."

"And who'd *he* take it from? Booth?"

"Who?" He turned to look at me with those big, dumb puppy eyes, mouth full and covered in crumbs. After a moment of silence, he smiled and turned back to the road as the highway became more congested.

The shack was smack in the middle of nowhere.

Theo kept groaning about wanting to stretch his legs and lay down, that he was tired of driving. After accidentally passing the closest rest stop, he took the next exit just to see where it headed. Houses dotted the road for a few miles until we hit a densely wooded area. After several minutes of taking what looked to be the oldest paths we could take, we stumbled upon the shack.

"I'm not sure this is safe," I told him, but he was already getting out of the car.

He pushed the door open, knocking the toes of his boots on the door frame to shake the dirt off. I followed suit. The shack was almost empty, an old futon and coffee table the only objects that took up considerable amounts of space. I flopped onto the futon, hooking my arms around the back with a sigh.

The seemingly collapsing walls riddled with cracks made it feel messier than it actually was. Almost all of the windows were completely gone, and the rest had dangerous shards of glass sprouting from the frames. Weeds and moss made their way up through the floor, covered in a dense blanket of dead leaves. For a moment I considered what kind of animals or poisonous plants could be lurking, but my relief of finally being free from that oily metal box of a car washed those thoughts away.

Theo sat beside me and craned his neck back until the curve of his skull hit the top of the futon's back, shutting his eyes. I watched as a tuft of hair in his face tickled between his eyes, his nose crinkling in annoyance. I'd told him before to cut his hair, that his bangs were uneven, but he insisted that it was too stylish to change.

He grinned when he caught me looking. "Like what you see?"

"You're so stupid."

He laughed and crossed his arms, looking out of one of the busted windows.

"If we stay here long enough, we could probably watch the stars for a bit. It's not too cloudy."

"Is that really a good idea?"

"Who knows? I just don't feel like leaving yet."

I idly pulled at my sleeve. He had urged me out of bed with a deathly seriousness, sounding as if I dawdled for a single moment the ground would fall out from under me. And now, with *that* in the trunk, he wanted to stop and stargaze. My jaw started to ache from clamping my teeth down with a ferocity born of uncertainty and anger.

I felt Theo pinch at my sleeve himself, tugging at it. "You're gonna stretch it out if you keep doing that."

I said nothing as his hand moved from the sleeve to my palm. It was colder than I had expected. Maybe it was the stress of the situation, or the raw bundle of fear in the pit of my stomach that refused to rest, but I felt little as Theo braced his hand against my back and reached up to touch my cheek.

I couldn't register his expression. Jaw clenched but lips soft, eyes boring directly into me. Red blotches of light filtered onto his pale face like Charon's Mordor Macula, his few freckles mimicking distant craters. He studied my face in a daze, running his thumb across the group of pores near my nose to the hollowing of my cheek.

He had me while Portishead droned from his phone's speakers and a cyclobenzaprine headache started to creep in through my eye sockets. I silently cursed myself for taking a muscle relaxer earlier while he whispered curses of a different nature. I lied with my arms around his back, transfixed by how the pulsing in my forehead matched the beat of the music. I briefly wondered if I would suffer the same fate as the person in the trunk, and if Theo would kill me in this same position—hovering over top of me, with hands around my throat instead of on either side of my head.

To be honest, this is what I had wanted for a long time. Maybe not in this specific setting or under these circumstances, but I wasn't going to turn down the opportunity. That was probably the biggest issue—I let him destroy all of my standards.

"You need anything?" he asked me from the edge of the futon once it was over.

"No." I balanced my cigarette between my lips for too long and felt the filter getting soggy with spit. He waved his own up and down, up and down with small juts of his jaw.

He looked down at the futon as I pressed the butt of my palm to my closed eye. Sometimes countering the pressure of these headaches with more pressure offset some of the pain. All I heard for a solid minute was vibrating bass, tinny metal, and Beth Gibbons' muffled mewling from the phone. I took one last breath before reaching over and crushing my cigarette into the chipped coffee table. With a loud crack, Theo twisted the cap off of a new water bottle and poured it on his shirt before handing it to me.

"To, uh, clean yourself up."

I stumbled as I dizzily made my way to the bathroom with only the light of my phone. I looked at myself in the mirror: disheveled, flushed, and lips swollen, but I recognized a fear in my eyes I wasn't even aware I was feeling. Should it have bothered me more that my first time with someone I'd been pining after was in an abandoned shack on the run from God knows what? Probably. He'd never expressed any interest, and now... this. Despite it all, the pit of my gut felt warm and soft and sweet, all of those dangerous enamored feelings rolled into one lump of sticky trash. I stared at a dark mark forming on my neck before wiping myself down the best that one can with a wet shirt.

"Hey. Are you scared of me?"

Theo spoke up only moments after I came out of the bathroom. I was more focused on the condom he must have unceremoniously threw on the mold-coated floor while I was cleaning up. After a moment, something dawned on him, and he rubbed the back of his head and sighed.

"Sorry, that question's harder than it sounds."

I rubbed my forehead and opened my mouth wide, but no sound came. I gritted my teeth as Theo looked up at me in silence from where he was still seated. After not getting a response, he prodded further.

"Noah," he cooed, leaning forward and focusing on me. "Are you alright?"

"What I want to know right now is," I started, putting my clothes back on as I found them on the floor, "why you never showed any interest before now."

"I didn't?"

For as ditzy as Theo consistently proved himself to be, this was a stretch even for him. He never showed romantic interest in anyone; he was too dense for the subtleties of romance. I was the last guy I expected him to pursue. I eyed him carefully as I finished buttoning my pants, trying to find some sort of crack in the mask I was starting to think he was wearing. With an indignant click of the tongue, I turned my head from him.

Theo reached out from the futon and held my wrist. "I'm sorry for dragging you into this. It'll be alright. We'll get home and everything will be normal again. Just bear with me until then. Please?"

I looked down at my wrist, held up only by his grip. "Do I have a choice?"

Theo stared up at me, eyes full of pity and something that said *no, you don't*. He craned down and kissed my knuckles. But no matter how gentle his voice was or how soft his touches were, something dark was radiating from him that I couldn't pin down. I hoped it was just my imagination, but I wasn't an idiot.

Despite it all, I felt a fondness douse my entire chest cavity when I looked at him. His smile was so weak, his cheeks awkwardly tugging his lips up at the corners. If he trusted me enough to bring me along on this ride to Hell, then I felt I had to be willing to protect him and ensure that he got there. He could hardly make decisions of any weight on his own. I was the only one who could help him at this point.

"Sorry, I'm probably acting weird," I mumbled. "But I'm happy that this happened." With a hand on the back of his skull, I brought his head to my chest for emphasis. "Really."

"Don't worry about it. I know how you are." I focused on the feeling of his breath between my ribs as I watched far off clouds threaten to blanket the sky.

When I first started to wake up, I couldn't place where I was. My entire body ached, right arm numb, and all I could smell was dirt. I tried to turn on my side, only to realize I was pinned to the futon by a sleeping Theo on top of me, cutting off the circulation to my arm.

I could hear robins singing in the trees shielding the shack. A dense fog settled at the floor of the forest, the moisture making its way into the shack and dampening anything it touched. Seeing everything now in the daylight, the shack seemed to have been abandoned for even longer than

I thought. It was a miracle all of this soft wood didn't come toppling down on us in our sleep. Among the mildew were purple wildflowers popping up every few feet from the door to the wall. Pushing Theo off to the side, I sluggishly rose from the futon and stretched my arms like a weed sprouting out of a pile of garbage.

I grabbed my glasses off the small table and wiped the condensation from the lenses.

"Hey, Theo, get up." I nudged his side with my foot every few seconds until he began to stir. He took a sharp, deep breath in through his nose and groaned.

"What time is it?" He reached into his pocket and pulled out his phone. I wasn't sure how he could read anything with the screen cracked the way it was. "It's only 7:30. Can't I sleep some more?"

"No," I told him as I picked his jacket up off the floor and launched it at his face. "We shouldn't stay in one place too long. And how did you sleep without that jacket? It's freezing."

"You were warm." I could hardly believe how matter-of-factly he said it as he shrugged his jacket on.

"You say the most embarrassing things."

"I don't think it's embarrassing. I mean, you asked."

I looked at him over my shoulder for a moment before heading for the door, pushing it open. "Let's just get going."

The naked branches of the trees filtered sharp, jagged shards of light onto the roof of the car. I dropped myself into the passenger seat with Theo not too far behind, ducking in and turning the key. A flurry of crows made a quick escape at the sound of the engine. The first thing he did was crack the back windows because the smell from the trunk was starting to creep in. I slid my hands into my fleece-lined sleeves while Theo tapped something into the map on his phone and docked it on the dashboard.

"Why'd you only set the destination for 95?"

"So we can get back on it without getting lost?"

I sighed and leaned back into the seat. "So you really don't know where you're headed."

He didn't say anything as he drove away from the shack and onto the road. Every time the GPS would speak up I thought it was him about to give me an explanation.

"Can you at least tell me when we're going to stop driving?" I asked, arms crossed and tapping my finger against my bicep.

"I'm not sure. Once it feels like we're far enough."

"We drove for *eight* hours yesterday. We'll be in Montreal by the time you feel like we're far enough away."

Theo pulled up to the worn out ramp, the GPS mocking me and telling me *you have reached your destination*. He reached out and gripped my knee, rubbing the side of it with his thumb.

"It's just…" His face tensed as he clenched his teeth. He was never one to bite his tongue. "Just stay with me a little longer?"

"I mean, I'm not going anywhere. Even if I wanted to, it's not like I could just jump out of the car."

He turned his eyes upward and nodded to himself, as if confirming with himself that I couldn't jump out of the car.

Theo quickly realized that there was only so much we could talk about after how much time we spent together yesterday. He'd make comments about stupid billboards or license plates, but after a couple hours, he was completely silent. We stopped once for gas, and I watched as Theo anxiously picked at his nails as the tank filled.

Whenever traffic slowed under fifty miles per hour, he'd reach over and hold my hand or my thigh without looking at me. A few times he gripped my hand with such strength that I wondered if he really thought I would find a way to leave before we reached wherever we were blindly headed.

"Uh… Is something bothering you?" *Other than the body in the trunk, which didn't bother you before.*

"No, no!" Theo swatted his hand in the air with urgency, looking over to check my expression. "Don't worry. Everything's fine. I guess I'm just tired."

"Huh." I kicked the empty Icee cup on the floor between my feet. Even if it was an obvious lie, there was nothing I could do to make him tell me. I propped my arm up against the window, rested my head against the bony pillow, and tried to fall asleep.

I woke periodically, finding that each time another half hour had passed. At 3:23, I noticed that we weren't on the highway anymore.

"Is it time?" I asked, stretching my neck.

"Yeah, I think so." His voice was feeble and defeated. "Looks like we might be able to find some deep woods over there."

Another half hour, and we were in a forest filled with pine trees. The pine needles were encased in ice, and with each strong gust of wind, I heard some of that ice topple to the ground. Even after turning off the engine, Theo sat and stared blankly at the dashboard. I got out and tucked my hands between my arms and my body to try and keep them warm while I investigated the area.

It was a dense forest, and we were deep enough in that we had to form our own path with the car and hope we didn't hit any trees. The soil was soft, probably from recent snowfall that had melted. I kicked through the thick, downed branches and tried to find an area that I deemed decent for burying a body, as if I had any idea what piece of dirt was better than the next.

I went back to the car and opened the trunk, finding a shovel and multiple black trash bags. The stench was overwhelming and nearly knocked me to the ground, but I was thrown back to sense when I heard Theo throw the door open and stumble out of the driver's side, the gun from yesterday in his hand.

"What are you doing!?" Theo gasped out with more fear in his eyes than anger. He raised the gun until it was facing me.

"I was just getting the shovel so I could start digging." I tried to speak as clearly as I could with a gun pointed at my head. But Theo swallowed hard and bit his lip, his aim not wavering.

"Theo. Don't." I tried to look into his eyes to calm him down, but his focus was frantically darting. I held my hands up in surrender. "I'm here for you, right? I'm trying to help."

He was shaking, and I could hear the metal of the gun clanking against a ring on his finger. "I don't want to. I didn't want to. I thought this might happen last night, but then I—"

"Wait, you were going to *kill* me after sleeping with me?"

"I don't know! I brought you to help, but I started getting worried. I didn't think it would be like that. I didn't think that I'd…"

"That you'd care?"

Theo's arm lowered a fraction. He nodded, looking away in guilt as he tried to collect himself. "But I did! That's what matters, right? That's why I kept driving. I wanted to spend more time with you."

He was near tears in absolute confusion as he covered his face with his hands, the side of the gun pressed against his cheek and temple. "Noah, I'm scared. I don't want to go to jail. I'll be on edge every single day until the cops show up at my door. I can't live like that."

"We can think of something. Just put the gun down. Killing me isn't going to stop that."

"I know. I knew since last night that I wouldn't be able to hurt you." He tried to force out a laugh, but all that came out was a weak puff of breath as he shook his head. "Does that make me weak?"

"Does that even matter?"

Overwhelmed, Theo sat down onto the ground, resting his arms on his knees and dropping his head. I was pacing back and forth, trying to make sense of every last moment we spent together.

"Why did you kill someone in the first place?"

"I don't want to talk about it," he whispered.

"Don't I deserve to at least know that much?"

"I said I don't want to talk about it!"

Theo's grip on the gun tightened, and there was a faint echo of his voice in the trees as a group of birds flew away. Seeing him angry was more terrifying than anything else that had happened. He hadn't ever mentioned anything warranting murder ever since I met him. He was never angry at anyone or anything.

I thought that he just avoided conflict. As I went over our friendship in my memory, I had to wonder if it should have caught my attention. Should I have done something differently?

I was focused on the damp earth when I saw Theo raise the gun out of my vision. This time, it was pointed to himself. I lunged toward him before I could think, and in the midst of the yelling, pushing, and pulling, a shot went off and shook my eardrum with such force that I wondered if I had gone deaf. I squeezed my eyes shut until the terrible buzzing stopped, panting and shaking as I gradually came to realize the bullet hadn't hit me. When I gathered the courage to open my eyes, I saw Theo on the ground beneath me—body limp, eyes wide, and with a hole above his eyebrow.

I felt my tongue hit my teeth and my throat vibrate as I yelled his name over and over, but I still couldn't hear anything. I steadied my hands on the ground on either side of his head, my right hand quickly becoming slick with warm blood. I tried my best to avoid looking at the chunks surrounding his skull like a bursting halo. I hovered over top of him, frozen in shock, until the muscles in my arms fatigued and couldn't support me any longer. I sat next to him and tried my best to wipe the blood from my hand on the ground.

My mind raced with static. No thought I had was willing to be pinned down, and I found myself at a complete loss. As my hearing gradually came back to me, I could hear the wind slipping through the pine trees with low howls and a single bird squawking somewhere within them. The wind pushed Theo's hair across his forehead, but he didn't squint and push it out of the way.

It was then, with my fingers going numb, that I realized he wasn't going to wake up.

I thought of what he would have wanted me to do. I pushed myself to my feet and made my way back to the open trunk. I was afraid of feeling the weight that was in the trash bag, but at this point, I couldn't stop. I knew, even when we first left, that after I saw what was in the trunk, any possibility of turning around and leaving had disappeared. It would make it too real. Grabbing the shovel, I started digging near Theo.

I clearly underestimated what was necessary to dig a grave. I managed to make a shallow one before my body started to ache. Hauling the bag out of the trunk, I dragged it over and kicked it into the hole. I didn't open it to see who was in it. It wouldn't have made any difference.

I packed the ground on top of them with the shovel with contempt, taking out my frustration with each smack.

After taking the keys from his pocket, I placed Theo in the trunk with great care, trying not to twist his body into any particularly unnatural position to get his lanky limbs to fit. Sliding into the driver's seat, I pulled the seat forward and adjusted the mirrors. I lit one of the menthols Theo left in the cup holder and took in a long breath, a breath longer than any of the ones I allowed myself to take in the last thirty six hours. Starting the car, I began driving in complete silence. I had no destination in mind and no desire to stop. I only wanted to spend a few more moments with him.

Melanie Czerwinski

@mel_czer

The Exorcism at Queen's Landing

If I had to pick a place in that village where everything started, everything from the supposed demonic possession to the sighting of the lake monster, Mussie, I suppose you could say it was Queens' Landing, but that wouldn't be fair. That quaint hotel on the shores of Lake Ontario in the village of Niagara on the Lake was built in the Georgian style of the English monarchs who frowned on anything out of proportion and balance. There was plenty out of balance there that weekend, but the architecture was contrived in mellifluous equilibrium. The grand entrance possessed four symmetrical columns that opened to a reception area floored in marble, so nostalgic of my British heritage, with no traces of French intrusion, and it seemed perfect, as though nothing could go wrong there. The charming gardens entwined with vast labyrinths of Velvet Green Boxwood and Wax Myrtle outdoors, and the English bedrooms indoors, with ruffled duvets and a four post bed in the bridal suite where we spent our wedding night, could never be blamed entirely for the unexplained events.

I must attribute the odd happenings that warned of turbulent times to something else, something foreign to the town.

It was springtime, almost summer, and along the street where hanging petunias spilled from the iron lampposts, the smell of English lavender, the perfumeries, the beeswax candles and the gardenia soaps from the shops along the street tickled my nose in the morning as I went out for a stroll, but by late afternoon, the restaurants imbued the entire village with the culinary aromas of roast duck and pan seared salmon with rosemary, simple pan fried potatoes that should have made the beginnings of our matrimony nothing short of divine.

My wife, Lucienne, was always a woman that oozed fertility. She had wide hips and large breasts and a vespine waist and not a sign of aging at 35, and though I'd always been a bad judge of character, I was certain that she was the woman of my dreams from first the moment I saw her ice skating in Ottawa. Her leggings moved like awkward scissors then, and her trunk advanced stiffly with every thought of hers seeming to cling to the idea of not falling, and the way she held her gloved hands taut to the side rail of the rink hooked me right there on the Rideau Canal, where beneath her, two white figure skates made linear cuts of shaved ice. When she came in and sat on the wooden benches and loosened her skates and took down her scarf, I saw her perfect lips that had paled in the cold air immediately blush the deepest pink, and I wanted to kiss them right there.

I suppose I married her much too quickly, proposed on our second date, actually, and it would be fair to say that we rushed into things, but I've always been a man of intensity, and there was something about her energy, too, that sucked me in, grabbed me by the throat and screamed to me that I must not let this woman get away like I had with my college sweetheart, the only other woman I've ever loved, Charlotte Cooper, who, sadly, broke my heart by running off with my roommate and former best friend, Horacio, from the rugby team. Charlotte had said that I was too intense.

Now I was more certain than ever that no other woman but Lucienne could make me happy, and I had to have her, possess her.

The wedding was set exactly four months from that winter evening on which she said yes without hesitation. We were married at Saint Mark's Anglican Church and proceeded to the reception at Queen's Landing, where we would spend the night, and in the morning, leave for our trip to England. Yet, in all honesty, we'd already fornicated at least twice a day, every day, since the day we'd met, to the extent that Lucienne had contracted a bladder infection otherwise known as honeymoon cystitis, only it was before the honeymoon. The infection traveled up her kidneys and she became disoriented and had to spend half of the time we'd known each other in the hospital, hooked up to an intravenous line of antibiotics, although in no way did this unfortunate turn limit our sexual activity. I should've known that her fits of passionate delirium in the hospital ward would extend their proclivity toward all things dramatic.

When I first arrived at the hotel on the day of the wedding, it seemed there was some sort of convention, a religious retreat, perhaps. I checked in before Lucienne was with me, of course. She wasn't even in Canada. She was staying in the States, just across the border, with her aunt Lisette, who'd married a Jewish neurosurgeon by the name of Arthur Gelden. She was going to cross the Queenston-Lewiston Bridge around noon with Lisette and Arthur, and meet the wedding party before the ceremony.

I was walking about the spacious library off of the lobby when the events began. It had a mahogany table and leather upholstered chairs, books bound in burgundy and deep greens. There were two clergy members standing near the expansive windows. The thin one was wearing the usual black pants, black shirt, and his white collar was stiff.

The heavier one appeared to be a bishop. He wore a black cassock cinched with a silk scarf red and wide, and he was carrying a bag not unlike the black leather medical bag that Arthur Gelden carried around with him, especially when he was looking for a reason to leave a family party early.

The priests didn't look so out of the ordinary themselves, but it became obvious very quickly, that something at the hotel was gravely wrong. I waited for my bride as the priest and bishop walked from room to room, examining the frames on the wall with great attention to detail, checking behind doors and listening to the end of the receivers of the phones, when no calls had been made.

"Father," I asked, "is something wrong?"

"Have you not heard the voices?"

"I just arrived."

The priest in black looked at the bishop, shaking his head. Then he extended his hand, patted me on the back as my rugby contemporaries did in college, and he told me to be careful, said, "The devil is always present. Do you reject Satan?"

I nodded, said, "I do," though I was not a particularly religious Anglican, and thought that the Catholics put a bit too much power in the church.

It was as if the bishop in the red and black vestments had read my thoughts precisely then, because he looked at me with a direct stare, and he said, solemnly, *"Roma locuta causa finita est,"* before he walked away from me, proceeding out into the foyer and searching behind the velvet curtains that draped the windows in a grand and picturesque style. From my years of studying Latin, I was able to translate his words to mean that the church has more power than ever.

That was the first moment I wondered if marrying a Catholic from the French province of Quebec was perhaps something I should've thought through a bit more, but I wrote off my hesitation to my unrequited fickleness, and my pendulous mood swings that my mother, God rest her soul, had often accused me of from a very young age, and I waited for my bride with only the usual wedding jitters.

My brother told me when Lucienne arrived, though I did not see her in her dress before the ceremony, and at this time, my hesitation was magnified, not simply brought on by cold feet, but by something far worse. A growling noise terrific and deep had twice resonated from the bookshelves in the library where I stood waiting for Lucienne, and I wanted to call back the celebrants at once, to ask them if it were some sort of cruel prank, maybe part of the theatre presentations of George Bernard Shaw that were performed at the Royal George Theatre down the street.

I began to bite my fingernails and pace about the room.

I had hollowed tiny crescents into my nailbeds, biting them with abject neurosis, even drawing blood from my index finger, when my brother, Grant, called me out of the library to start the ceremony. When I caught sight of Lucienne, she looked so lovely in her brocade dress that revealed her shoulders and breasts in a way that could not be called demure, creating elegant lines that accentuated her hips and buttocks, and all of my fears at that time were immediately repressed.

Later, when the guests had left and we were sitting on the bed in our room, I told her that I would not allow her to rest until the sun came up, that I would make love to her nonstop until check out time, but I did not.

A pervasive thought entered my mind at that moment, about the sounds I'd heard, just as one of the pictures, an artistically mediocre oil painting of a sailboat nondescript and banal, fell from the wall behind the bed.

Instead of undressing Lucienne as I should have, I told her about the clergy, the way they were milling about the lobby, and what the bishop had asked me, what he wore, and I told her about the growling I'd heard in the library.

"Hugh, there are ghosts here, *Mon amour*," she said, teasing me with her bilingual sentiments. She laughed, said, "The war of 1812 saw the death of many soldiers, and their energies haunt the village, sometimes to extreme."

Then she said that she wouldn't be surprised if the priest and bishop had been called to perform an exorcism, said that over 400 of them were performed each year in Quebec, and, unless I were the one possessed by a demon, I should not worry.

After a while, when she'd been drinking Frangelico and vodka, and I'd had several pints of grapefruit infused craft beer, we were laughing so hard about the way her aunt Lisette and her husband, Arthur, danced, that she almost fell off the bed. Then she suddenly changed the subject. She said something that planted the smallest seed of doubt in my mind. I'm sure she'd intended it to be endearing. It was an idea that began as a subtle interjection, and grew, juxtaposed to thoughts of our interminable happiness, and it caused me tremendous anxiety, and a nervous twitch in my legs.

She said, "I hope to heaven that you never leave me, Hugh, because if you do, I won't allow you to go. I'll be one of those crazy broads that attaches herself to the heel of her man, biting and screaming like some rabid and insatiable animal, as he tries to limp away. You would never do that to me, though, would you, Hugh?" She made a puppy face and when the expression fell away from her eyes, she laughed boisterous and crude and she put the brown, friar-shaped bottle of liquor to her lips, and drank a large gulp.

I started to feel my throat tighten right then, was done with my beer. I developed a suffocating, clenching, gripping, tightening, around my neck, that forced me to loosen my collar and gasp for breath.

She trounced, intoxicated and sloppy, on my lap, slobbering at my cheek, rubbing her palm over my pants, between my legs, telling me how lucky she was to be loved by me, and I realized how in those statements she'd devalued herself. I felt then that I'd mistakenly married a sure thing, whom I thought had been a hard to get *mademoiselle* with the attitude that her shit didn't stink, the usual uppity, *right shoes, right bag* francophone Quebecois from Montreal that I had an unfortunate predilection for, bordering on an obsession. I'd never had much luck landing the type, though, as Charlotte had proven. Before me was a girl who'd told me only hours before exchanging vows, how she'd grown up in a mobile home near Muskrat Lake. And her family, the way they cussed, their grammatical expostulations of backwoods slang. What had I dove in to?

When she told me how much she needed me now, I felt the pressure of those words, their implications, and I backed away.

There was time to go back, we could have the marriage annulled, not consummate our vows.

But I couldn't think as far as tomorrow, because from the walls, I heard the growling again.

It was that of a savage animal, emanating from beneath the bed, only when I threw off the lace duvet and searched beneath the bed, nothing was there.

"What's wrong, *Mon amour*?" She smoothed the hair on the back of my scalp where it itched the most from my haircut at the old time barber shop the day before, the one next to the apothecary, and I thought I might, in fact, crawl out of my own skin. "You do love me, don't you? We're married now, forever. Can you believe it? It seems impossible, Hugh."

"Tell me about the spirits." I rose from the bed, walked to the window.

She came up behind me, pawing at my waist. I threw open the windows, drew in a cooler breath. On the dresser, the maid had left a bottle of champagne on ice, two strawberries, and a plate of dark chocolate squares topped with white chocolate cameos. She tried to place one of the chocolates on my lips, but I rejected her advances.

"These chocolates carry the face of a very important woman, Hugh."

I was certain that her drinking was affecting her behavior, and probably my indecision. But it was late, too late. I'd married this woman in haste, and she suddenly looked less attractive to me, less youthful, and quite desperate. "Oh?" I offered a weak smile, eased down into the pinstriped chair at the dressing table.

"This woman here," she said, pointing to the cameo, "walked twenty miles through rain and thistle brush, to warn the British soldiers of an impending attack from the Americans. The battles that ensued here were some of the bloodiest in Canadian history."

"The lady on the chocolate, eh?" I asked. Reluctantly, I took a bite. I'll admit that she was a history teacher, and I was embarrassed that I didn't know more about my own heritage, but she sounded mad, simply mad, the way she was pointing to the little face on the candy and licking it in a lascivious gesture.

"Laura Secord," she said, advancing toward me again, lapping at my neck, "is a national heroine."

"Right." I turned my head, away from Lucienne. I'd heard it again, from beneath the bed, the growling, that guttural and bestial sound.

"*Mon amour?*"

"I think we need to take a walk."

"Yes, let's," she said, always eager to please me. It was already more than I could stand. Why had I been so foolish? I'd been caught up in my conquest, but now that the thrill was subsiding, here I was, tied to a woman I barely knew, forever, for life. She took my hand, but before we left the room, I picked up the phone, called the front desk.

"I'd like to make a complaint," I said. "There's been a lot of unusual noise here."

The operator told me to hold.

Lucienne tugged at my sleeve, kissed me on the neck, tried to pull me away from the phone. As she wrenched at my hand, I stared at the mirror, examining the man before me, and the longer I stared, the more I heard that gut rumbling awful noise, until the mirror began to shake, and it fell from the wall where it hung.

"Let's go," she said.

I dropped the phone, grabbed her hand. She led me out into the hall.

When we walked out of the hotel, the evening was humid, there were wisps of fog on the lake, and the cicadas rattled my inner ear like a bad case of tinnitus, unrelenting, humming a sound that was impossible to subdue. Lucienne was still drinking, but she'd finished the monk-shaped bottle of liquor, and now she uncorked the champagne. She removed her shoes, drinking the champagne from the bottle while crossing Ricardo Street, and she ran in her nightdress barefoot to the park beside the lake.

I chased her, called after her, now more concerned for her safety than my sanity.

"I know a lot of ghost stories, Hugh. Let's go on a ghost walk."

"Lucienne," I said. "Did you hear anything unusual in the room?"

"You mean a spirit?" She winked, mocking me.

"It sounds crazy."

I chased her out to the gazebo beside the lake. There was a collection of spiders stringing glistening whorls of silk that clung dewy to the wooden supports, and the moonlight made silvery the lake where the houses beside the hotel sat amongst gardens full and bloomed.

"Lucienne," I called. "Please come back."

"I want to show you the river monster. Follow me."

"Be reasonable. There is no monster, no creature. There are no demons—"

But the terrible growl came again, this time from the lake. It rumbled the water in wide ripples that traveled circumferentially outward from a point illuminated beneath the moon.

"There's something out there," she said.

"It's nothing. Just a big fish, or a log, a boat."

"There aren't any boats out there now, *Mon amour*. I was serious, Hugh, about the spirits. I think they're closer to Fort George, though. Where many of the soldiers died. Maybe we can see them from the lake."

"I heard something in the hotel, in the room, a growling sound."

"It could be a river monster. I have to see it. Look, Hugh—out there."

She ran across backyards of private homes along the lake, beyond the lighthouse. She scaled a chain link fence and narrowly missed being bitten by a chained Rottweiler on the lawn of a white home bordered by pink hydrangeas. I couldn't stop her before she climbed into a boat, docked in the marina between two sailboats. It was an eighteen-foot

Citation with an inboard and outboard motor. I didn't expect her to know that most of the people who lived there left their keys right in their boats, but she started it right up, and I had to leap from the dock to catch her, because I'd had to run around the home with the vicious dog and around the neighbor's yard, over their fence, before she had the boat untied and was headed out onto Lake Ontario.

"Lucienne, stop this. You've got to turn this boat around. We're going to get arrested," I screamed.

The beacon from the lighthouse shined to the east, disappeared in a roving silhouette.

"Over there. I see it."

She was right. Out of the lake rose two humps that rippled the water, shook the boat. A thump beneath the starboard side made me call her name, grip my seat.

Lucienne laughed, sipped the bottle of champagne.

"You think this is funny?"

"I think it's beautiful how we're still just getting to know each other, and yet we have our whole lives." She offered me the bottle.

And there was that sense of suffocation again, the fear of intimacy that trapped me. She drove the purloined boat further out into the lake. My breathing quickened, my heart thumped inside of me. I'd heard of Mussie, otherwise known from my campfire days as Hapaxelor, a silvery brown monster that inhabited Lake Muskrat, Lucienne's hometown, but I'd never believed the stories, the ridiculous tales about the twenty foot serpent with three eyes, flippers, a pointed crest, thick skin resembling an alligator.

This was Lake Ontario, not Lake Muskrat.

Lucienne spun the boat in circles. Then she drove straight, full speed, creating wake that thrashed the cattails in an island of grass near the shore. "Nobody's really afraid of Mussie, Hugh. You seem spooked. Let's be wild, free. We have our whole lives."

"No, Lucienne. We don't. I made a mistake."

"What do you mean, *Mon amour*? I'm just having some fun."

"Will you quit it with the French? Take this boat back." I tried to take the wheel from her, threw the green, glass bottle of champagne into the lake.

And then, another noise.

This time, it wasn't a growl. It was an ear piercing, beeping noise, and it was coming from inside the boat.

"That's the depth finder," she said. "Turn it off, or someone will hear."

"They can hear the motor for miles, you fool."

"Hugh." She looked hurt, and her face furrowed into a dejected pout, but she was beyond drunk.

The sonar device for catching fish was still alarming, detecting something at four hundred feet deep from the boat, and rising, slowly. It was something about twenty feet in length.

"We need to get out of here, now, Lucienne."

"It's because my father told you I don't live in Montreal, isn't it?"

"What? No, I didn't know that. I'm just learning about our differences, and I think we may have been too hasty."

"You had to take French in school, too, Hugh."

"What does that have to do with anything? I said I've made a mistake."

"He told you I'm not a school teacher, didn't he? That I'm just a waitress, a bad one, too. I drop everything, spill coffee on folks." She started to cry now, which I hated. Her tears made her makeup run black and terrible in the moonlight. Her face was already pale.

I looked around the lake, back at the depth finder. Whatever was down there was rising toward the boat, fast. And then, something came up to the surface, briefly. It was leathery, with a single tooth. I grabbed the wheel of the boat, pushing Lucienne out of the way, drove the boat forward, full speed.

"I'll get a better job, Hugh. I promise."

"We'll talk about it back at the hotel. We need to go."

I looked down at the water. Whatever I'd seen was gone, the depth finder was silent again.

"*Je suis pleine*, Hugh." She rubbed her belly.

"You mean, *j'ai trop mange*. I ate too much, too. At $250 dollars a plate, I'd be upset if you didn't. We can work it off in the room." I winked at her, saying whatever I could to get us out of there. I heard the growling around us again, that inescapable, rapture of hell, from beneath the boat.

"No, Hugh, I mean, *je suis pleine*." She had a wicked smile that spread a coy curlicue over her cheeks, satisfied, as though she'd succeeded in trapping me, even if I was ready to speed away, realizing my mistake, my fear.

I stopped the boat in the middle of the lake. There was a cool wind from the southwest, creating swells, and the boat did not want to be still. I grabbed her by the throat and pushed her down to the floor. "Stop playing games."

"That's no way to treat a pregnant woman," she said, gasping.

"You're not pregnant, you're drunk." I slapped her face, then returned my grasp to her neck, encircling it tighter, harder. "I thought I knew you, but we don't know a thing about each other."

"I am pregnant, *Mon amour*. All that time in the hospital. The morning sickness, the vomiting. It wasn't just a bladder infection."

"We're not going to have any baby, do you hear me?" I slapped her harder. My child would be an imbecile. I wouldn't have it. "We're going to go to a doctor, to take care of this."

She writhed there for a minute, struggling, her arms thrashing left and right on the floor of the boat, soaking her nightdress with the windy swells. I stopped, briefly, when a bright light appeared behind me, illuminating her face weathered and terrified, and the area where my hands around her neck had turned her lips blue. The two celebrants were behind me, pulling up close in a tugboat, its bell clanging loudly, echoing, on the otherwise silent lake. The only other sound now was the sloshing of the water against the sides of the boats.

The bishop was standing at the bow of the small dinghy. His hand shook, brandishing a cross with an outstretched arm. He said, "Take hold of the serpent."

Lucienne called in French to them, as if she knew them, or knew something I didn't. I couldn't understand what she was saying, but she kept going on in French, that foreign corruption that spewed from her tongue now.

The priest held a lantern, and the bishop proclaimed, "She speaks in tongues."

Lucienne saw something in that light, screamed in English, "The fire!"

"Yes, my dear. That's it. The Holy Spirit is with you," said the priest.

The bishop held his arm out farther, straighter, in front of his face, holding the cross firmly, though it trembled, and the dinghy approached the boat, even closer.

The bishop said, "I cast out the demon, the evil one. Do not punish the innocent before us, but be rid of Satan, the dark master."

Lucienne looked too scared to get up, and she was still gasping. Her throat made sucking noises, and she convulsed in a pool of lake water, lying there. Something in the waves flapped against the surface, a fin, a tail, maybe. I turned, looked over the left side of the boat, and the right, where it slipped back under the surface, disappeared a smooth illusion beneath the waves. I faced the bishop, gripping my chest. Lucienne grabbed my face, pulled me down, screamed in French, then English.

"You wanted me, Hugh. You wanted this. You pursued me. Now you pretend to run from women like me, but you're walking, Hugh. You want me to chase you, play your little game, your little chase." Her eyes swelled wet and red from the fire of the lantern that the priest held over me. Those eyes were hot, glowing. Her hair was dripping, her face too, with beads of lake water and perspiration salty and hot. Then her voice came from the pit of her stomach, like that macabre low pitched rumble I'd been hearing. "You're not running, you're not. You're not even walking."

"Take my hand," said the bishop. "The church does not intend to punish that which the evil one possesses. Take my hand."

"She's just trying to get attention," I shouted, turned back to Lucienne, said, "Stop it. Stop it."

"The fire," said Lucienne.

The bishop said, "She see tongues of fire! My dear, the Holy Spirit is with you."

"You called them, didn't you?" I shook her chest, put my hands around her neck again. Her eyeballs drained backwards, falling away from her anger, and then her globes were motionless.

Behind me, the bishop's voice cracked, "I invoke the power of the Redeemer, and cast out the Prince of Darkness."

I turned my head around, shouted at the bishop, "She's afraid of you."

The priest, who was soft spoken and quiet until now, said, "Young man, Satan is afraid of this man."

The bishop continued, holding the cross over the boat, over at Lucienne, and me, chanting, "Banish the evil forces, and destroy them from in those he holds in his clutches."

Then a low, oppressive noise drowned the voice of the bishop. It was not the depth finder, nor the rich and velvety growling sound I'd heard. Whatever I'd seen in the lake was gone. A blinding light, white, then red, rotated, cycled on and off Lucienne's face, the water. The scent of the fish and soaked flotsam on the water mixing with Lucienne's sweat, her perfume from the shops, was dense. I was breathing it heavily, and Lucienne was still breathing, too, shaking beneath me where I straddled her. Waves tossed the boats in the wake of a larger vessel now. It approached, slowly, a red boat. It was the coast guard, and the police.

I looked up, said, "Shit," then down at Lucienne.

She thrashed, groaned, "Hugh," but she did not open her eyes.

"Promise me. There's no baby," I screamed at her, but she was unresponsive. "Promise me now. I swear to you, I'll kill you."

"Take your arms off the woman, put them in the air where we can see them," said the policeman, close to the stolen boat now. The officer's partner threw out the bumpers, and with agile celerity, climbed aboard. I put my hands up, allowed them to take me.

I heard the priest protesting, explaining that any of the spirits could've caused the demon to take shape, said that it could've been the ghost of the abused woman who haunted the restaurant on Queen Street, or the spirit that took on the Olde Angel Inn, where witnesses frequently experienced patches of cold against their skin, brought out by the British Captain Swayze, who was murdered by American soldiers in the basement. They described similar ghosts, at various locations, emphasizing the innocence of the possessed victims, insisting, but the police seemed concerned with their formalities only, took me at once to the station, booked me, and I sat in a cell there, alone, until Lucienne came and had me released.

Lucienne had regained consciousness immediately, but she did not remember the incident at all, and after being checked by emergency medical staff, who attributed it to syncope, or passing out, and a subsequent hypoxic episode, along with a bad case of alcohol intoxication, she seemed more concerned about me. The lack of oxygen and inebriation with alcohol had erased all memory of the event, and the clergy had not accused me of malevolent intentions. I was free to go, though my hesitations about the marriage remained. We returned to the hotel that night, where I did not make love to her, but I spoke to her in a fluent and luxurious French that came to me without explanation, until she drifted off to sleep.

Melissa Franckowiak

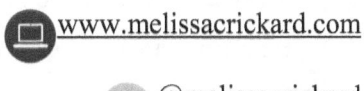

www.melissacrickard.com

@melissacrickard

Treasure for Sea

The boy jumps back as the lid slams shut. A chest of treasure hangs in his arms. He pushes open the back door and races up the steps, fumbles for his key. Panic blossoms, the key rests inside. Dread fades to relief, develops into irritation, and lands on acceptance. Apartment 4B is unlocked, again.

His sock covered feet skid to a stop, assisted by frayed linoleum. Coat and boots arranged in a heap at the door. He makes room at the kitchen table; scattering long-gone papers, Chinese cartons, leaded weights, and gaging scale. The treasure box is stained and torn, its reds faded pink, whites now yellow, and blues turned gray, no matter, it's the contents he's after. The lid flips open revealing a tattered cardboard world attended by pastel currency, festive buildings, and silver-toned markers. A single die remains, once there were two. Doesn't matter, the treasure is his.

Surveying his bounty, he's interrupted by small voices from the front room, distinct yet the same, both too loud. Fright dispatches his brief victory. He snatches the box and sprints to the source. Finger to his lips, he whispers an invite to little sis and her dolly, would they like to play? Sis shakes her head no and Dolly stares back. It's teatime.

He retreats to a corner, crushed but not beaten. Great explorers prevail, conquering bitter cold, cresting overfull dumpsters, and avoiding enticement from 1A. He opens the lid to shield his tears and studies the board. His gaze travels over trains, dodges a policeman's whistle, and lingers on the cell. The jailbird's resemblance is eerie.

The boy pinches a green dwelling between finger and thumb. He peers at the cube and surveys his own, a docket that includes the ratty couch that doubles as a bed and a solitary chair. Dishes molder in the sink, their odor and presence evidence of meals gone by. He glances at the bathroom and tries not to reflect of the horrors residing on the scarred sink.

He flings the emerald house from his fingers, regretting the strike. The plastic cube zings off Dolly, who doesn't seem to care, but Sis whirls a curse in his direction before she can grab it back. From the bedroom, Mom groans but Eddie continues to snore. Minutes pass, thirty, catastrophe evaded.

The boy abandons his game, first seizing the shoe. He awards Sis the token and she counters with tea. Tap water in a paper cup. They sit together, still like Dolly. Souls touched in solace, trusting mom and Eddie will wake, but fearing when they do.

Patrick Gibson

www.patrickwgibson.com
@pwgibsonauthor

Shore

Going out in public is risky. Sometimes, people see me. They don't know how to react, or if they should react. Stella says it's disruptive. But it only happens sometimes. Mostly, if anyone notices me at all, it's more like they feel something off. Like a bad smell or sudden current of cold air.

An old woman gets on the bus and she sees me. She sits in the handicap seats and turns to look over at me and Stella sitting in the front-facing seats beside her. She rears back like something bit her and crosses herself. She knows what I am.

Stella's doing that thing where you pretend you don't see anything at all. But the old lady, she's having none of that. She reaches over with one gnarled hand and grips Stella's knee. I want to slap her hand away, but I can't touch her.

I don't know if it's the clear plastic scarf covering her fluffy white curls or the way her black eyes are sharp like a crow's, but the old woman reminds me of someone and I don't like it. I don't like to remember.

See, the problem is Stella wants me to remember. But I'm afraid if I do, it's over and I'll have to leave. I'm pretty sure, given the way I ended up here, my life before this was shitty and I don't know what comes after. I'm going to stay here for as long as I can, thanks.

"I can help you," the old woman hisses at Stella.

Stella smiles that tight smile you give to strange people. "Thanks, but I don't need help," Stella says. I grin at the old woman and she takes her hand off Stella's knee so she can fish a cross out from under her coat. She kisses the cross and under her breath murmurs a prayer.

But she's not going to give up. "I know someone. A priest. He can help that poor child cross over to where she belongs."

Stella smiles that hard, tight little smile again. I can feel the tension in her body. Because while Stella would be thrilled for me to leave now, she can't let me go. Not until we figure out what the fuck I'm doing here.

I imprinted on Stella like a duckling. That's what she says. Honestly, we're just guessing here. It's not like people know anything about this shit. But this is how it happened.

I died.

Fine. I was killed. Someone beat the shit out of me and then strangled me and left me.

And then, I just kind of hung around, looking at my body on the riverbank. It started to snow and I watched it fall into my open eyes. My skin was all weird, mottled with purple and my eyes got cloudy. I don't like to think about it.

Stella found me. Or her dog did. They'd been running along the trail, when her dog came running up to my body and Stella yelled out, "You better not be rolling in something dead, you little shit!" She's still working on forgiving herself for that even though I told her it doesn't bug me.

I hid behind a tree and watched her puke and cry and shake.

When she'd calmed down enough, she called the police. The cops came and milled around my body. One of them wrapped a foil blanket around Stella and led her to a cruiser to warm up in. I followed.

The old woman on the bus tries again. She gives me a look and her expression moves from wide-eyed fright to a kind of dog-eyed sorrow to stern. There's that memory again, tickling at my mind, but I shove it back. Not today.

"I know it's hard to let go. But for yourself, for her, you must." The old woman rummages in her square black purse. She brings up a brochure. "This is the church." She presses it into Stella's hand.

"You're very kind, but I don't know what you think I need help with," Stella says.

"I can see her. She's wearing a purple sweater and too much eye makeup."

Stella breathes in sharply. People turn to look. Nothing like a little drama to make the ride more interesting. I know she's tempted. But I can't say anything. I'm too angry. How dare this old woman think she knows what's best for me?

The day after Stella found me, I was waiting in her living room. Her dog, Buddy, remembered me right away. He just rolled over and showed me his belly, while his tail thumped against the floor.

She screamed when she saw me. Then she said something about trauma. Then she refused to look at me. "I don't have time for this," she muttered and turned on her laptop. She was talking to someone on a video call. I don't know. She does something with computers that's really boring.

But the guy she was talking to, he saw me. "Your niece staying with you?" he asked. And she lied. She said yes. He was so happy because he'd been worried about how Stella was coping with finding a dead kid. At the end of the call, Stella closed her laptop and turned to me.

"Why are you here?"

I shrugged "I don't know. Maybe because you're the first person to give a shit about me." When she'd been sitting on the trail, waiting for the cops, she'd said, over and over, "Oh, little one, what happened to you?"

"Who are you? The police want to know."

"I don't know. I don't remember anything."

For the first few weeks, Stella worried she was having a psychotic break. She got used to me. She named me Kore. I don't really need a name, but it's important to her.

We figured shit out. Like, how she can give me things. We ended up building a little shrine. She put up a framed copy of the sketch of me the police put out. No one ever called to say, "That's my girl." I went into the ground nameless.

I picked out the candles. "Are you religious?" Stella asked. I just liked the way Jesus and his mom looked on them. Anything Stella puts at the shrine, clothes, food, it appears in my world. That's our theory. I'm on a different layer, let's say. For things to pass through, we need a little magic.

The old woman, she doesn't know any of this. I'm just wrong, maybe evil.

Stella doesn't really want me here. She wants me to have a name and a family who misses me. She wants justice and to know I was loved. I don't know if any of that's going to happen.

Once, on a bad day, Stella banged the table and howled, "Why you? Why not him?" And she burst into tears.

Her husband died a couple years ago. He was young too. I was younger than that, but all of us should get to be old. She'd have him back if she could. Instead, she has me. I follow her around like a balloon on a string.

I want to tell the old woman to go to the old rail bridge. There's a dead girl her priest can help. I saw the girl once and my skin crawls to think about her. Because she wasn't like me. I'm pretty sure I look like I did when I was alive. But this girl, she's skin and hair hanging on bones. She smells like death and all she can do is wail. Stella saw her too. I think Stella sees her in her nightmares.

"Let her have peace," the old woman says to me. She's holding out her cross. What am I, a vampire? "The priest can help you. He can help you rest."

The reporter, Jo, wouldn't like that either. Jo visits Stella and she can see me too. She tried to touch me the first time she saw me and when her hand went right through me, she fainted.

Jo and Stella argue about how they'll explain it if I do remember everything and the police solve my case. Anonymous tipster, Jo always says. But Stella's not sure. She worries people will find out they talk to a ghost and then Jo will be laughed at, her career ruined.

Other times, they just make dinner and drink wine and talk like friends. I pretend they're my moms. I think that's what's happening, even if Stella was married to a guy before. I tease Stella about Jo and she blushes and tells me to mind my own business. Once, when Stella went to get another glass of wine, Jo shook her head at me and told me I was a cock-block. I'm the worst dead foster child.

"It's wrong to let her stay," the old woman says to Stella. Stella presses the button. It's not our stop, but she's had enough. Me too.

Here's the funny thing about being dead. You'd think you'd care less about everything, but I'm angry all the time. What a fucking cheat. My life is better now than it was when I was alive. No one wanted me and some asshole killed me. It burns me up.

"LEAVE MY MOTHER ALONE!" I scream at the old woman. Some of the passengers hear something because they're looking around all wild-eyed. But that doesn't last too long, because the inside lights flare bright blue and go out with a pop and then the bus shudders to a stop.

Smoke starts to pour out of the engine. The driver throws open the doors and starts yelling for everyone to get off. The old woman is the first one out. She runs like she's forty years younger.

People mill around looking at the flames shooting out from the bus. Stella and I slip away and start walking home.

"Your mother?" Stella asks, laughing a little. Oh good, she's not angry at me for losing my temper. It happens. I broke all the glass in her house once when I got mad and screamed.

I shrug. "Close enough." Then, because I have to say it, "You're not exorcising me. I'm not---" I don't know how to finish that. Ready? Done?

"I know." She holds out her hand, even though I can't take it. "Come on. Let's go home."

Bess Hamilton

www.besshamilton.com

@bess_p_hamilton

@besshamiltonwriter

Medina

It was particularly cold for an early March morning. The sun peeked shyly from the clouds, draping a single dust beam across the length of the bedroom. Medina was already awake, wide-eyed with a perfect smile that discounted the rest of her alabaster skin. It was a special day for Medina; a day she knew all too well. Her smile did not grow any wider, even though her birthday was upon her. She had other concerns to fret about. She was awaiting Mother.

Mother was always interfering in her life. She always wanted to know all about Medina's misgivings. Where was Medina going so late at night? Why was Medina failing her subjects? What was that musky smell in her underwear drawer? Who was that boy with the charming brown eyes and fast motorcycle that always seemed to call at a quarter to nine each evening? When did Medina start fancying dark mascara and brighter-red lipstick? What happened to her little girl who used to wear pig-tails and cute chiffon dresses without worrying about boys, and always minded her Mother? These were the kinds of interrogations Medina loathed, and just knew that this day would be no different. No, this day would be far worse than all the rest.

The bedroom doorknob jiggled, then went silent. A bronze key was inserted into the lock, and wrenched the tumblers while turning clockwise. Outside, it started to lightly rain. Medina continued her smile, preparing for the onslaught, as Mother opened the door and entered the room.

Mother was a lanky woman, as tall as she seemed so prematurely aged. What were once golden locks now dripped with graying circlets, tucked into makeshift curlers on top of her creased brow. Mother's choice of garb this day was simple: an olive dress with patchwork near some of the faded seams. Slowly and with great, painful effort, Mother crossed the threshold, and turned on the light switch to her right.

"Don't you ever knock, Mother?" Medina said cynically, her smile still dancing on her face. Mother did not respond; she just approached Medina's desk and began to straighten the multitude of novelties and dust-covered trinkets that threatened to spill about the ashen-colored laminate below. Medina stared in wide-eyed amusement.

"So, you are going to give me the silent treatment?" Medina declared. "On my birthday, no less? The one day I expect you to lay the compliments and judgments as thickest as thieves, yet you choose to ignore me?"

Mother turned in her direction slightly, reached down to fetch a bauble once purchased by Medina when she was thirteen—it was a faded cherry lip gloss, now molded after years of use and misuse, and frank abandonment—and pitched it into the overflowing trash can beside the desk. The rain fell harder now, enveloping any sunlight that once entered the bedroom earlier. Medina would not be discouraged; she knew she had her Mother where she wanted her. The rain just amplified her mood.

"All these years, Mother, you cared enough to tell me how I should feel," Medina began, still beaming that perfect, red-lipped smile. "You lectured me on who I was allowed to be with. Who I was allowed to date. The tone of makeup my skin was permitted to wear. The length of my skirt. If I should go out. When I should come home."

Mother moved on to the dresser now, clearing her path from the desk and upturned hamper filled with ripped blue jeans and dank, half-sleeved, hair band t-shirts. Atop the dresser were several picture frames, some in shattered fractals due to frequent mishandling. A specific picture of Medina and Mother lay in tatters, neatly piled to the back left corner of the white oak dresser. Mother carefully gathered the pieces together and placed them in the trash can along with the rest of the rubbish, ignoring Medina's declamation.

The rain fell even harder. Mother moved to the window and closed the drapes, sealing off the outside world. Medina's auburn hair splayed gracefully across her shoulders, and she smiled broadly at her Mother.

"You know, Mother, I'm an adult now," she said. "I'm eighteen. I no longer have to do as you say. I no longer have to listen to your rules. I am free to do as I wish, even if you do not approve. I can date who I want. I can wear as dark of makeup that the boys like me to. I can go out late and come home later. And there is nothing that you, or anyone else, can do about it. Nothing."

Mother turned from the window, and looked directly at Medina, seeing her for the first time this morning. Medina smiled, knowing that she would finally acquire her Mother's attention.

"I deserve respect, Mother," Medina stated. "I demand it. Say something!"

Tears formed in Mother's eyes, and her brow creased even further. Mother reached for the light switch, dampening the only source of brightness in the room. The raindrops pattered passionately against the siding, pawing at Mother's heart like a harpist does to his strings.

"Happy Birthday, Medina," Mother croaked with a tearful voice. "I love you immensely, and miss you even more. How I wish you were still with me." With a sob, Mother turned the bedroom doorknob, opened the door, and vanished from the darkness.

Medina continued to smile, as only a portrait on the wall could.

Sal LoMonaco

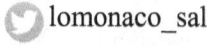 lomonaco_sal

salvatore.lomonaco.5

A Special Bond

The strange and very sad case of Emma G— came to my attention during a tour of the Amundsen Psychiatric Hospital in 1953. I was soon to replace Dr. Goodson there as Supervisor, and he led me through the corridors of the facility, pointing out the rooms for patients and resources for treatment. As we were passing the dining hall, he turned my attention to a patient of special significance.

"Her name is Emma," he said, in a tone that could only be described as woeful. "She was admitted last year in a dreadful state of depression. Her son, Lt. Frank G—, had been captured by the North Koreans and was held in a POW camp."

The woman might have seemed in her forties, if not for the tight hair bun that added ten years to her. She sat by herself, enjoying either a late breakfast or early lunch, not easily distinguished
at that time of morning.

"She hardly looks depressed," I observed, for she was voraciously attacking her meal, her enthusiasm apparent in the rapid downing of pancake pieces and in shoveling to her mouth a
succession of spoonfuls of hash browns. Somehow she managed a smile while chewing.

"It's in sharp contrast to what you would have seen three months ago. She ate reluctantly then and had to be forced out of her room. When her husband brought her to us, he mentioned she
was devastated, as she had read in the papers that North Korea routinely

starved its prisoners to death."

"Is she better now because he survived?"

"She's better now because I appealed to what her husband said was a special bond between her and her son, her love compounded by almost losing him in childbirth. Frank was rescued by an emergency Caesarean."

"What did you say exactly?"

"More than I should have, in retrospect. I told her the bond she had with her son was special, and she should keep her thoughts positive. I said she must eat—it would be for him."

"She looks healthy enough now, though perhaps eating too much."

"When I said she must eat for him, I meant of course he would want that, would want her to thrive. But in her desperation she thought I meant he would thrive by her eating. She began to eat with the enthusiasm of an expectant mother eating for two. She is doing so well now, I haven't dared to tell her the sad truth that Frank is dead."

"He was starved to death after all?"

"Actually, no. There was a report from a soldier who had been in the camp with Frank. While other prisoners wasted away from malnutrition, Frank somehow kept his weight, even gained some. He stood out among the still living skeletons around him."

"You don't believe—"

"I'm not sure. It's a choice between weird science and coincidence."

I noticed Emma had finished a dessert, and she was reaching for a second dessert on her tray.

Goodson suddenly looked discouraged. "If I told her the rest of it, I'm not sure what the effect will be."

"Told her what?"

"The North Koreans figured Frank must be stealing food, or that the guard in charge of distributing the meager daily calories must be favoring him. Both the guard and Frank were taken aside and executed, just one day before that POW camp was liberated."

Alan Meyrowitz

Dark Fork

Jonathan closed his eyes and listened to the water. Whenever he crossed Dark Fork on the big chestnut log his grandfather had felled across the stream, Jonathan did this, stood halfway across in his self-imposed darkness until he imagined he was falling into the roiling creek below. The water spoke to him then and he would be on the brink of understanding the liquid language at the point he was sure he was toppling into the flood, then he opened his eyes to find himself still quite upright above it, and the water was just noise again, with sunlight flashing from its surface and glimmering among the rounded stones in its depths.

Dark Fork was named not for the shadows that cloaked it, except at the height of a summer day, but for Jonathan's great-grandfather, Edwin Dark, who first claimed the steep and stony land along its upper reaches, where the creek, that in some lesser country might have been termed a river, roared and tumbled and plunged down a narrow bouldered gorge, so sequestered from the sun by the high shoulders of mountains on either side, that most who knew of the place called it simply, The Dismal.

The original human inhabitants of the area believed the Dismal a way into the underworld, a place inhabited by ghosts and demons. Most would not even drink the water from the stream that flowed out of it, so they suffered Edwin Dark, pale and solitary, an outcast even among his own kind, to occupy his chosen acreage unmolested, and when he seemed to thrive in a place where there was scarcely enough sun and soil to grow a scraggle of corn, they decided that Edwin must be himself a devil. It was a mystery, even to his own descendants, how he ever persuaded the woman named Dream Eater to share his exile, or why her people would have allowed their improbable union. It had happened, they all agreed, for they were the proof of it. Each generation made up their own stories about Grandmother Dream Eater, but the stories were more revealing of the imaginations of a clan of inveterate story-tellers than of any verifiable history.

Edwin's children had children before the Darks knew by name the nearest neighbors of Edwin's own race, and saw little of them but their chimney smoke on a winter morning when the trees were bare and one could see for miles down their cove. The Darks were pleased to be apart to themselves, preferred their own company above all others, and unless they were in search of necessities like tools or wives, the Dark men tended to avoid places where humans gathered in numbers. They were honest, hard-working, not mean nor cruel nor greedy, but by no definition sociable. They were to a soul passionately contrary to any thing ordinary. Their forbidding, inhospitable slice of the earth seemed to suit their perverse natures, and for two generations, the broader world left them to it.

~

Jonathan Dark, his elders decided, would be the first of his clan since Edwin to stay long and far from the forbidding country of their hearts. He had a scholarship to the state university campus in Asheton, a thriving Appalachian tourist town - the Darks counted it a city - two ridges away across the mountains south and east of Dark Fork. Jonathan, thus became the first among his kinsmen to be burdened with great expectations beyond discovering and becoming fully himself. He did not protest, but he did not wear his load easily. He suspected he might be about to participate in a life where he was passably good at all manner of things he'd just as soon not be doing.

Jonathan never anticipated, much less sought the complications Starblossom Dorn brought to his young life. She came to their homestead with her father who was inspecting a small tract of timber he considered buying from the Darks. Jonathan, as boys will do, made fun of her name. She told him her mother had named her after the weed that grew around their steps the morning she was born.

"What about you, then?" she said.

Johnathan puffed himself like a lovesick toad, "I was named after the son of a king."

"You're too scrawny to carry around such a heavy name," she said, all solemn and serious. "I bet I can beat you to that tree yonder."

She pointed toward an old pine across their yard and Jonathan took off for it. In spite of his head start, the girl touched the scaly trunk first. Star laughed, and Jonathan stalked off into the woods, breaking any branch within reach he thought he could manage to damage. He never looked back. He was afraid she would see his defeat glistening on his cheek.

Jonathan never saw Starblossom Dorn after that until he rode the bus down to the county high school at Poplar Spring and glanced covertly at the dark haired girl assigned the seat next to him. By then she had blossomed into a ripening young woman. The sight of her slender neck curving up between her collar and her hair rendered him breathless as had their childish race.

Starblossom caused Jonathan to be suspended from school in his junior year, though she never knew it. He watched her from afar, never daring to speak to her or of her to anyone. She for her part, appeared to him to be oblivious to males. Her only observed conversations were with friends of like gender. Boys were watching her, though. Jonathan knew that. It rankled him that some would speak of her as if she were a young ewe or heifer awaiting inspection at an auction.

When Jason Embers nodded toward Starblossom in the lunch line one day and snickered, "My boys, would I like to poke around in that now," without a thought Jonathan hit him square in the face. Jason was by good measure the heavier, and would have doubtless wiped the floor with a Dark mop, but his tray flew at the blow, Jason slipped in the wet of his spilled milk and went down, cracking his head on the corner of a bench and rendering himself unconscious.

Fortunately, no lasting damage was done. Jason spent a few days at home recuperating from a mild concussion, and both combatants were suspended from classes for a week. When they were allowed back, after stern warning and threat of permanent expulsion in the event of recurrent hostilities, neither ever mentioned the incident again, and their friends feared to bring up the subject in their presence.

The altercation only insured that Starblossom remained studiously oblivious to both participants. When Wallace Keller, son of Poplar Spring's only practicing attorney, took a polite fancy to her, she encouraged his attention, and Jonathan gave up whatever hopes he might have nurtured to ever find her favor.

~

No real road led to Dark Fork from anywhere. A rough track barely fit for a tractor provided their tenuous connection with the larger world. The school bus stopped where this trail met the county road two miles down the mountain, and Jonathan and Starblossom would walk home from there. Every day, she would charge ahead, daring the boy to keep her company, and Jonathan would hang back, content to catch a glimpse of his heart's desire at every bend. After a mile, he passed her house, and his long legs made much better time the rest of the way.

One rainy September afternoon, Starblossom slipped getting off the bus and fell sprawling in the mud, ruining the new dress her mother had made for her, and sending her books and papers flying across the puddles.

The driver, a scrawny old bootlegger named Silas Sykes, looked out the door, "Youns all right there?"

Starblossom limped to her feet, wiped futilely at her muddied dress, and with tears tracing down her face, answered in a voice trembling with more rage than hurt, "Don't you mind, Sykes, I'm fine."

Jonathan stepped down behind her, Silas closed the door, and the younger children pointed and laughed as the bus pulled away. Without a word, Jonathan gathered up the scattered books, put them back into her bag, started to hand it to Starblossom. When he saw she was obviously in pain, he shouldered the bag himself and held out his hand.

"Don't you touch me, Johathan Dark," she spat at him, angry for no reason except he had been witness to the spectacle she had become.

"Touch me, then. You're hurt." he answered, patting his unburdened shoulder.

Starblossom put her hand on his shoulder and they hobbled away up the path until Jonathan saw a sapling small enough for him to cut with his pocket knife, but stout enough to keep his companion upright.

"Wait." he whispered. And she did. When he handed her the walking stick, carefully cut and trimmed, they went on. Starblossom didn't protest when he put out a hand once or twice to steady her on a rough patch, or when, once they reached her house, he carried her books to the porch.

"If you'll wait up on me, Monday," he said, "I'll tote your bag for you to the bus, only if your foot ain't better, understand."

Starblossom offered no thanks, nor any word at all, but met his gaze and nodded. Jonathan went on his way back to the Fork, sensing that something had changed between them, without any vaguest notion of exactly how or what. The two days between Friday and Monday seemed longer than long to him. He thought Starblossom, muddy and lame and angry at life, more beautiful than ever he'd seen her.

~

Jonathan Dark never meant to hurt anyone. Even after it was over, he could not have said who took advantage of whom. When Starblossom invited him on a picnic, a picnic and an afternoon in her company was all that was in his mind. They spread their food on a flat boulder beside the little waterfall above the crossing log over Dark Fork, just beyond sight of the path. The first kiss was Starblossom's idea. The second was Jonathan's. Their swim in the pool at the foot of the fall was a mutual inspiration.

Afterward, they lay in the sun drying on the warm rock. Starblossom's taut breasts and flat belly drew Jonathan's sight until nothing else could be seen. He reached over and lay his hand in the hollow just beneath her ribs and felt her life under his palm, throbbing and surging like the stream beside them. When she took his hand in hers and pushed his fingers down to the moist nest between her thighs, they turned to one another and lost themselves in mutual exploration and ecstatic discovery.

~

Jonathan Dark was walking Starblossom Dorn home one last time, although this trip, there were no books to carry.

"What have I done wrong, Star?"

"It's Starblossom. You know that. My name is Starblossom."

Jonathan, frustrated almost to tears, willed his voice steady as he answered, "But you were my Star and I was your Jonny until graduation. Then all summer you treat me like a stranger. What did I do?"

Starblossom's face flushed with what looked to him like anger. "You're going off to college. I'm staying here. Everything will change now."

"But I'm coming back. We talked about that. We've given ourselves. I'll always come back to you."

Starblossom shook her head, looked away, wiped her face with the back of her hand. "Go and forget about me. I would only hold you back."

Jonathan would have said more, but Starblossom ran on ahead. "Go, and leave me to myself!" she shouted at him without looking back. She was afraid he would see her terror streaming down her face.

Jonathan threw up his hands in a futile plea for heaven's intervention, but he did not run to catch the fleeing Star.

It wasn't anything you did, my dear foolish boy, Starblossom screamed inside herself as she ran, *It was what we did that day. It was our only day. I wish now there had been others, that I could carry more sweet memories to my end."*

When she reached her house, Starblossom kept running. Nobody was out to see her pass and call her back. She ran until her chest ached and her stomach hurt. She pressed against it with her hand. Her stomach always hurt of late. She kept it bound tight so the life growing inside her wouldn't be public. She walked on until she came to the log across Dark Fork, and once across, she left the path and made her way up to the little waterfall that had witnessed her undoing. She was still sitting there, adding her own dark tears to the flow of the Fork, when Jonathan crossed the creek later. She heard him stop and call her name. She didn't answer, though she half-wished she had after she heard him walk on up the path toward his own Darks.

~

Starblossom was not ignorant of her own body. When the moon had turned twice without drawing her blood, she confided her fears to her friend Martha. Martha whispered the name of Lizzie Charon. The old herb woman lived up on a high bald accessed by no road at all, just a single trace for two-legged or four-legged beings afoot. Starblossom knocked on the door and waited. While she summoned nerve to knock again, it opened suddenly and a wizened face appeared out of the shadows beyond. Starblossom would have turned and fled away home but two eyes bright and sharp as a hawk's nailed her fast where she stood.

Lizzie shaped something near a smile with her thin mouth, radiating unfathomable calm while she held out her hand. When Starblossom took it, Lizzie led the girl into her dark little house and sat her by the fire, then sat herself just before her guest, their knees nearly touching. Against the silence, as Lizzie's gaze searched her out, the flickering fire sizzled and cracked and sighed like a flock of starlings taking flight. Starblossom realized other eyes than Lizzie's were watching her from the shadows in a corner, throwing back at her the hot glow from the hearth. A large hulking bird, an owl, perhaps. She couldn't tell. Her heart raced and her breath shallowed on the verge of panic, then slowly, slowly she began to settle into Lizzie's peace. She stilled and waited, patient beyond expectation.

After a minute or an hour, the Herb Woman spoke, "Was it love or lust? Did he force himself?"

For no reason she could think, Starblossom wasn't surprised that Lizzy Charon seemed to know without asking why she had come. She felt that she was seen through and through by this old woman, that there was no way now to be but honest. "I invited him in. Had he not been so willing, I might have begged him for it."

"And has young Dark refused his child?" confirming that Starblossom had left all her secrets at the door.

"He doesn't know, and I can't tell him. He would come to hate the burden of us."

Lizzie reached out and touched Starblossom's knee. A warm current welled through her, resolving in tears. Lizzie queried at a whisper while she leaned her face close enough that Starblossom could feel her breath, "And will he love you longer if you pluck from life the fruit of all his longing for you?"

Starblossom stared at the old woman. Lizzie drew back and shook her head, "That is what you want from me, isn't it? I can't give you what you've come for. You took to yourself a right-hearted young man. He wants no more than to be true to you. Deny him that, whatever you think it might cost him, and there will be no end in this life to his hurt or yours."

"But you don't understand," hissed Starblossom. "He's leaving Dark Fork."

"Then you best go with him if he does. Go or stay wherever, you will be together."

Starblossom stretched out her hands, knelt like a supplicant at a chancel rail. "Please help me. Please??

Lizzie took the young hands in her old ones, and stood, her own eyes glistening with tears when she said, "I've given you what I have. Let your Jonny give you what is your right and his."

"I can't. I can't. I will not hold him back from his life." Choking on her sobs, Starblossom ran out the door. As she fled across the yard toward the concealing trees, she heard Lizzie's door slam behind her. Whether it was the old woman, or the wind that closed it, Starblossom didn't know or care.

~

Lost in the song of the little waterfall, Starblossom played her visit to Lizzie over in her mind. The old woman had helped others, why not her? She knew Lizzie was right. If she told Jonathan about their child, he would abandon his dreams and stay to care for them both. But his family would judge she had ruined his life. The Darks kept long score. At every given opportunity, they would remind Jonathan of all he had given up, until at last he would come to agree with them that she, or any woman, was unworthy of such cost.

"No. I can't." she whispered to the gathering dusk. She took off her dress and folded it neatly on the rock beside her. Her sister had envied her for it, and could have it now. Then slowly, Starblossom slipped into the pool, and when she had accustomed to the chill, lay back into the dark water, and let the current carry her.

~

When he felt his vertigo build to certainty, Jonathan Dark opened his eyes. As he expected, he was still upright on the chestnut log. Below him, flashing amid sunstruck waves and ripples, the bright stones of the creekbed, and among them, brilliant under the morning, an object he recognized even before he fetched a branch from beside the stream and snared it to his hand. He held it a moment, dangling from its broken chain, the locket he had given Starblossom for her birthday, back in the spring.

"So, she thought no more of me than that," he said aloud to the day, and threw the trinket as far down the creek as he could. Then he hurried on to whatever might be left of his life. This seemed to be Jonathan's day for rejection. He had planned to tell Star today what he told his family the night before, that he had never wanted to go to university, and wouldn't. After a long silence, his father said, "You're old enough to be your own man. But you'll have to do it someplace else."

Jason Embers was working on a carpentry crew in Poplar Spring, building summer houses for rich people, and said there was a job there for Jonathan if he wanted it. Jonathan broke into a run. He didn't want to miss the bus to Poplar Spring.

Henry Mitchell

Monsters in the Cellar

"Don't go in the storm cellar—there's monsters down there," Momma always told me. But there ain't no monsters. Momma was always telling me them things to make me mind, me being an ornery kid and not easy to bring up. Like she told me be good or Santa won't give me nothing, though he never did give me much anyway, mostly old used toys like from a second-hand shop. And the Easter Bunny—that story didn't make no sense, some magic bunny leaving me a bag of jelly beans from the Dollar Store with the price tag still on. And of course, Jesus. I got more Jesus in one week than all the chocolate and Christmas presents I got my whole life. I guess Momma figured toys and candy wasn't enough to make me good, you know? But maybe Heaven and Hell would do the trick.

The monsters was like that, just another dang lie to keep me in line. Momma and Father Farrelly was always going over all kinds of sin, like stealing and lying and sassing back and saying Jesus's name in vain, and how Jesus 'n' Santa was watching me all the time and knew when I ever did any of those things, but the monsters was only ever about *one* thing: don't go in the storm cellar. I'm thirteen now and I know them things is all foolishness but still I never did go down in that cellar. Funny how the lies folks tell their babies stay with them.

Most boys like me had older brothers, and sometimes sisters, who explained things, and got them past the age when stupid things made sense. I didn't have no olders nor no youngers neither, being the only child. I figured things out myself, kind of late, no help from Momma. Momma was the only one told me anything after my daddy lit out.

My daddy went away when I was little. I remember he was a big man, and loud, but what he looked like I can't say. In my mind I see a big, black shadow, with no face, looming over me and Momma, and awful loud. Momma'd be loud, too, when they got at it, the way they did most days. I don't remember much more'n that, just Momma and Daddy fighting and me crying and holding my ears.

Daddy never hurt me, but he hurt Momma. Most times he slapped her, and that made Momma mad, though she never hit back. One time I know of he hit her with his fist, hard enough to knock her down. She crawled to a corner with blood coming out of her mouth that she wiped away with her shirt. I screamed and cried but Momma never did. Daddy raised his fist like he was going to hit Momma again and Momma lifted up her arm to protect herself. They stayed like that, not moving, Daddy with his fist raised up and Momma in the corner waiting for it, like they was posing for a picture. You know how you sometimes remember things like a picture, with nothing moving? That's what I see in my mind now, just that one picture, remembering what happened before and after but not able to see it.

Then Momma laughed, not like she was happy, but more like she knew what was coming and didn't care no more. I know she laughed, though I can't see it in my mind, just like I know Daddy never hit her again after that.

Then one day Daddy was gone. "He lit out," Momma told me, as best I can remember, me being four at the time. That made me cry to hear it, though I can't say why a man that made me cry when he was around still made me cry when he wasn't around no more.

The year after that is kind of blurry, but later years I remember was hard. "Daddy had a job in the mine," Momma said sometimes, especially when she spent her money on liquor instead of food. "The mine was hard work," Momma said, "but the pay was good." Those was the only times Momma talked about Daddy, when she was drinking. She sounded like she missed him, but I think she only missed the money. Momma worked odd jobs, cleaning and such, but mostly we lived off help from Momma's man friends.

It wasn't long after Daddy was gone that Momma told me about the monsters. She didn't go into a lot of detail at first. She didn't have to—when you're a little kid, you scare pretty easy. When I got older and started asking questions, Momma told me more about the monsters. They wasn't monsters like in the movies, zombies and such, but animals who lost their eyes in the dark and grown big. Momma said animals stay naturally small in the wild, where people and other animals hunt them, but in the cellar they live off of small animals that wander in and get eaten and the monsters just keep getting bigger. The older I got, the more she told me about the monsters, to keep me scared and out of the cellar. When I was ten I started not to believe her, because the stories got so crazy—six-foot-long raccoons with fangs, their eyes turned blind and milky white from the dark, who could find a body and kill him, just from smell and sound. I didn't believe it, but it worked anyway. I figured like even if there wasn't no monsters down there, what there was was just as scary. I stayed out of the cellar. Until today.

We put Momma in the ground this morning. There was me by the grave, and Aunt Clara, Momma's sister, and a cousin of mine, Aunt Clara's daughter Ellen, an only child like me who I didn't know too good. Aunt Clara looks a lot like Momma, only bigger and her face is younger-looking, though she's Momma's older sister. She doesn't look no happier than Momma ever did. It's just her and Ellen since Uncle Hap died in the mine, with Aunt Clara living off his union pension. I didn't think Aunt Clara had any man friends, but she did take in laundry for money. Still, Momma told me Aunt Clara did okay for herself, since *her* money didn't stop coming when Hap died.

Ellen looks a little like Momma, too, in her eyes and in her mouth, but a lot younger, of course. She looked like she didn't know who it was we was burying or why she needed to be there, but she never fussed. She wore a black dress that came to her knees but no hat with a veil like the one Aunt Clara wore. She looked kind of sweet, standing there holding Aunt Clara's hand, and I felt for her, being Aunt Clara's only girl, and no olders to look out for her.

The only man friend of Momma's who showed up was Father Farrelly, who looked to me like he didn't want to be there at all. Some years back when Father Farrelly'd come to me and Momma's house he was all smiles, chucking me under the chin and saying "my son" like *he* was my daddy, before Momma'd send me outside, saying "don't y'all come back for a while; Father Farrelly and me are talking about spiritual things." Yeah, *spiritual things*. All the sins they told me about at home and at catechism must not of been the whole list, and Father Farrelly and Momma had a few sins they kept between them and never talked to me about. Like I said, I had to figure things out myself.

Father Farrelly wasn't smiling today. He hurried through the Mass, hardly saying ten words about Momma, and he mumbled the prayers by the grave like he had someplace else to be. After he said the last words and blessed the coffin he lit out just like Daddy, if Daddy lit out. But I had my doubts about *that*.

Aunt Clara said she'd take me in, me being just thirteen and not ready to be on my own. Once Father Farrelly left she tugged my sleeve and said, "Let's go now, Dominick, no point in hanging back." I stuck by the grave, though, while the diggers covered it up, telling Aunt Clara to come by the house that night to collect me. I needed to get my belongings, I said, and besides, I had some things to do.

The cellar was outside, away from the house, set in the side of a hill. A *storm cellar* Momma called it, though we never did go there in a storm, not even when a cyclone came through when I was eight. Momma took me in the bathroom, wearing what she always wore when she wasn't having over a man friend, an underthing like a slip, that came to her knees and hung on her like a sack, all yellowish, though it might of been white at one time. She'd been drinking again, and she brought a pint bottle, half-drunk, into the bathroom and set it on the sink. Her eyes was deep and dark around the bottom like they always was when she'd been at her bottle, but with the storm coming she looked even worse.

We hunkered down in the tub, Momma at one end near the sink where the bottle was, and me at the other, the both of us hugging our knees while the wind blew around us and the house shook. When thunder boomed I flinched and whimpered, and after I did that five or so times Momma reached over and touched my hand for a bit. That surprised me, because Momma wasn't the touching kind, though it did make me feel better. When the lights went out I could still see Momma's face when the lightning flashed. Her eyes was round and she bit her lip as she rocked to and fro. In the dark I could smell her, sour, like sweat, and her breath like liquor. She moaned and mumbled the whole time, and I couldn't hear her too good over the storm, but I knew what she was saying. I was saying it too: *Holy Mary, Mother of God, pray for us sinners, now and at the hour of our death.* That night I believed Momma's stories about the cellar more than ever, if Momma was more scared of the monsters than a cyclone.

That was near five years ago, but even today, I didn't want to go in that cellar. I told myself there wasn't monsters there; they's just another one of Momma's lies, and I believed that was true, but going in there still gave me a bad feeling, like cursing *Jesus Christ*, which I know don't mean nothing. But Momma and Father Farrelly telling me all those notions about Jesus and sin and Heaven and Hell since before I could feed myself worked its way inside me. I wasn't going to talk myself out of them overnight. The monsters was like that, so crazy they couldn't be true, but standing at that door I was that scared kid in the bathtub. I picked up my shovel and tapped on the door and told myself, *Momma's dead, and her lies with her. Any monsters in that cellar, Momma put them there.*

Even after I broke off the lock I had to use the blade of the shovel to pry the door loose. The door creaked open, not a high, whiny creak, but low and slow, like a rusty hinge does that hadn't been opened for a long time. I listened, but didn't hear nothing. I picked up my flashlight and shined it down the stair. It was steep, but not long, just five steps. It wouldn't take much to drag a heavy load to the door and push it down. Even a small person, a lady, like my momma, could manage it.

The roof of the cellar was a lot lower than I expected. I had to bend down to get in. I couldn't see much, my eyes just come from the light. I shined the flashlight inside.

"The cellar," I whispered. The word fell out of my mouth like a rock, weighted down by a whole life of lies and a little kid's imagination. *The cellar is a cavern, big as a school gym—the cellar is filled with huge columns made of rock, where monsters, blind cave-animals hide—the cellar is all twisty little passages where the animals above wander down and get eaten by the monsters, who grow enormous on their bodies—the cellar stinks of dead things; the smell of it will kill you before the monsters do.*

I moved the flashlight around. The cellar was small, no more than a hollow in the hillside, barely ten feet deep, and not as wide. The air was cool and smelled of earth, not moldy or musty but clean, like a field just plowed. The walls was rock, the roof made of wooden beams set close together. The floor was made of dirt, mostly flat, but not all over.

There was a little hollow near one wall. That puzzled me, because I figured that if there was something buried here there'd be a mound to mark the spot. But then I realized that if I was to bury something that I didn't want found, I'd spread the dirt around to level the floor. I don't know if I'd of thought that the dirt would sink when the body broke down.

I put the flashlight on the steps to light the way. I poked the shallow spot with the blade of my shovel a few times before I started digging for real. I didn't dig long before I hit something that didn't feel like dirt. I cleared the hole out, then I got my flashlight and looked inside.

It was a skeleton, a human skeleton as best I could tell. I squatted down on my haunches by the hole, cursing, not caring if I took Jesus's name in vain. I cursed at my momma and all her man friends; I cursed at God and the whole world; I cursed and cried and rubbed my face 'til my face was muddy. I laid down on the dirt and cried, with the sound of my crying sounding hollow in the cellar.

It wasn't Daddy's skeleton. It was tiny, a little baby. I wanted to know if it was a little brother or a little sister. I wanted to know if I would of loved her, and played with her, and told her secrets, and helped her to understand that not everything Momma told her was true, and that some things was lies.

I wanted to know if one of Momma's man friends helped to put her there.

I laid on the dirt for almost an hour, then I covered up the hole and patted the earth flat. I went in the house to get cleaned up and to pack. Aunt Clara will be by for me soon. I'll live in her house from now on. I'll be okay. And there are things I want to say to cousin Ellen, who is much younger than me.

Charles O'Donnell

 www.charlesodonnellauthor.com/wordpress/landing-page

 @kozmickid

 @CharlesODonnellAuthor

Brother

I sensed the car behind me slowing down. I couldn't see who was driving as the car pulled to a stop next to me, but I saw a hand reach over and roll the window down a bit.

"You wanna ride, bro?"

I knew the guy driving was my brother's friend, though I didn't really know his name. I think this was the guy they called Ducks, but I wasn't really sure. I hesitated a bit, but the wind had picked up since I left the house, and I was only wearing a flannel over my t-shirt. I nodded and lifted the handle on the door.

Ducks's car was old; it had one of those big bench seats in the front. The cold vinyl that met my back as I sat down told me Ducks's car wasn't going to be any type of refuge from the cold, but at least I was out of the wind.

Ducks didn't ask me where I was going. It didn't matter; I wasn't headed anywhere, but I started to wonder where we might be headed.

"Remember that time we fuckin' fell in that pothole, dude?"

"What?"

"The fuckin' pothole, over by Timmy's house."

"Sorry, I..."

Ducks pulled his sunglasses down and looked over at me. "Holy fuck! You ain't Billy," he said.

"No, I'm Billy's brother."

Ducks laughed. "No shit, man. You look just like a little, tiny Billy. That's fuckin' crazy. So where you headed, Little Billy?"

"Nowhere, man. Just, ya know, wanted to get out of the house."

Ducks looked over at me again. "Crazy, man," was all he said.

We turned up onto Longs Hill. Ducks didn't say anything for a couple minutes. He played with the stereo, then pulled out a pack of cigarettes. He offered me one, but I shook him off.

"Where's your brother been, anyway?"

"Uh, out, I guess. I came home last night; he was out. Saw him Thursday."

"That's alright. No big deal. I'll catch him soon."

We were at the top of Longs Hill now. We would make our mom take this way home sometimes when we were little; we called it the rollercoaster hill because it went up and down real quick in this one section. She used to speed up a little and the shocks on her Olds would creak real heavy. Me and Billy loved it. Ducks sped up a little when we got to the hills. He must have loved it too.

"You like that, kid? Funny what you gotta do for fun in this town."

I just smiled and nodded at him. I rested my head in my hand, and looked out the window.

We came down the other side of Longs and Ducks made a right onto Painters. This would bring us back into town. I thought maybe he'd stop at the 7-11. I knew Billy and his buddies hung out there sometimes, so I thought maybe that's where Ducks was headed.

"Kid, you wanna do an 8-ball?"

I didn't know how to answer him; I wasn't sure what he was asking. I knew I had to answer though and I knew I had to answer right. But the words just escaped my mouth, "You mean like pool?"

Ducks just laughed and looked at me again over his sunglasses.

"You sure you're Billy's brother?"

I knew "8-ball" didn't mean pool. I thought about all the fights mom and Billy were having lately, how she's screaming at him about being on drugs, and how he's screaming back at her that she's crazy. I was starting to think maybe she wasn't.

"How old are ya, kid?"

"Fourteen."

"Fuuuuck, fourteen? You look older. You got any pussy yet?"

I snorted a little and shrugged. "A little." A lie.

"Man, what kind of brother you got, don't help you get none? You come see me. I know some loosey-goosey mommas gonna hook you up, bro."

I snorted again and nodded. "Okay."

"Man...fourteen and no pussy. Gotta –"

Ducks's eyes flashed up to the rearview, to the blue and red lights that were flashing behind us. "Fuck." He started to pull over in front of Lorie's Flowers and said, "Don't worry, kid. We clean."

We sat on the side of the road for a long minute. Ducks's hands were tight against the steering wheel. I'd been in the car once when my Uncle Dale got pulled over; he made me get his papers out of the glove box. I thought maybe I'd get Ducks's papers too, but he didn't ask.

From behind us a voice said, "Please exit your vehicle." Ducks threw his door open and stepped out. He was standing right next to the car. The voice behind repeated, "Please exit the vehicle." I didn't understand; Ducks was already out, until he said, "Get out, man. You get out, too."

I opened the door and stood on the side of the street. I could see Ducks's hands were spread across the top of his car, so I did the same thing. I saw the shapes of two men cross in front of the police lights. One of the men approached me, and started to pat his hand up and down my legs. "This ain't him," he said.

The officer standing next to Ducks said, "You seen Billy Taggert tonight?"

Ducks raised his eyebrows at me. "Nope," he said, and he stressed the *we* when he said, "we ain't seen him."

"You seen him?" the other officer asked into my ear.

"No."

I stood there with my hands on the roof as the officers shined their lights into Ducks's car. "You see Billy tonight," Ducks's officer said, "you tell him I was looking for him."

We got back into the car and Ducks took a heavy breath. "Fuckin' cops."

He started his car, and we headed down the street. We passed the 7-11 and we went down Main Street.

"You live up on Wooster, right, kid?"

I made a noise like a "yeah". Ducks turned up onto Cellantano. We pulled onto my street, and I pointed when we were almost at my house. I said, "Thanks, man," and got out of the car. Behind me I heard Ducks roll the window down.

"Hey, man...uh, if your brother's not around ever for some reason, and you wanna hang out, it's cool. You can just come around, and we can party if you want. Or whatever."

I nodded and just said, "Thanks, man" again. I turned around and headed up the steps to my house. Ducks waited until I was at my door, and then pulled away.

I stared at the door for a minute. I didn't think Mom would be cooled down yet, so I didn't want to go inside, but it was really getting cold now, and I still didn't have a jacket. Ducks's car was warm, but I didn't think it would be cool if I ran right back to him like that. I wasn't even sure if I wanted to. I could go to Mark's house, but there was still too much snow in the woods to take the cut-through, and I didn't want to walk all the way around.

I reached up and grabbed the handle to the screen door. I held it long enough without pushing the button that the cold started to hurt my hand, so I let it go again. I thought about all the ways Mom was going to scream at me again when I went inside. I thought about Billy and where he might be and why the cops were looking for him. I wondered if that had anything to do with Mom yelling. It wasn't fair if she was taking Billy's shit out on me, but I knew she had to be worried like me.

I reached up for the handle again and it didn't seem as cold this time. Nothing felt as cold; I was getting a rush of energy through my guts. It was time to step inside.

Mom was sitting at the kitchen table, smoking. She was still in her nightgown, but her hair was wet, so she must have showered and just gotten back into her PJs. She didn't look at me for more than half a second before she picked up her lighter and started flipping it in her free hand, banging it hard against the table each time. I opened the fridge out of habit and closed it again without really even looking inside.

I was about to walk to my room when mom said, "You seen your brother?"

I left my back to her but turned my head. "No."

"Well, if you see him, don't tell nobody. Don't even tell me."

With that, she stood up and walked past me to her room down the hall. I thought she'd slam the door, but it closed soft, softer than she ever did anything. I thought about her on the other side of that door and started to cry. The last time I saw her do anything soft like that was when Gramma died, when she went to her knees in front of the coffin and raised her hand up and touched it so soft. I thought of her on the other side of the door on her knees again crying over Billy and whatever he'd done.

I went up to my room and waited for something. I didn't know what I was waiting for, but I could feel it coming. I thought about all the things Billy could have done and all the things that could happen to him. He could go to jail, or maybe get shot. I thought about losing him and all the ways that would be bad and all the ways that would be good. I felt guilty for both. My mind drifted back to Ducks and the rollercoaster road, and then to Mom and Billy and me back when we were happy, back even before Dad left. I heard the phone ring and I heard Mom answer. I didn't hear her say anything, but I heard her slam the phone down, and I knew that something I'd been waiting for had come.

Dan Pullen

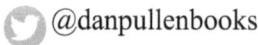 @danpullenbooks

Back Wall

What he most liked about the neighborhood was its quiet. It was, in that way, a typical sleepy suburb, ignoring most of the larger world's turmoil, going placidly along day by day, providing decent shelter and allowing its citizens to follow their own untroubled paths. At the same time, though, it was less than a half-hour from Philadelphia -- and less than two hours from Manhattan, if he desired to make one of his occasional visits there, visits that were more like clean tactical raids. And his neighbors, even if they knew who he was, had shown themselves quite willing to leave him to his own devices. It was not an obvious choice for the home of a reasonably successful playwright, yet for C. K. Hauser it had done perfectly. So, in the small room on the third floor, where the slanting slate roof made the dimensions a little more interesting, Hauser would sit facing the rear window. When he would glance up from the computer, perhaps letting the precious beads of inspiration condense in his mind, it was to see the top of the house across the back alley, some unremarkable foliage rustling in the breeze, and a blue, cloud-streaked sky. Few distractions. Few noises or voices, especially during the day when the neighbors' children were at school and the husbands (and some wives) at work. True, there was always Saturday, when the lawn mowers growled away for hours, and Sunday, when the potent smell of burning charcoal and broiling hamburger, the steady chatter and ball-bouncing, made it difficult to concentrate. But that was all right. Hauser had adjusted, he told himself, as any intelligent and civilized person should. He worked five days, then rested the next two -- which, he also told himself, was a better deal than the Great Playwright in the Sky got when he designed the very first sets. And Hauser's wife, Roberta, was pleased with his working arrangements, for it allowed her to invite guests on the weekend or slip away with him to a museum or show. Yes, it was all very satisfactory.

On a Monday morning, in late spring, nearing noon, Hauser had been at work for a few hours. His desk was a long slab of butcher-block wood that rested solidly on a pair of two-drawer filing cabinets. And when he was temporarily stuck -- whether the problem was the choice of *le mot juste* or the satisfying resolution to one of his characteristically ebullient and complicated scenes -- Hauser could turn to the small bulletin board on the wall to his right and gaze fondly at a few select clippings. There, for example, was the usually intractable critic of *New York*, giving in to Hauser's farce of lustful cosmopolites, *But Never In the Pantry, Baron Dear!* There was the no less intractable critic of *The Atlantic*, yielding before the effortless frivolity of *Ormolu*. A Boston critic rhapsodizing about *Edward Etheridge: or, Life Among the Defenestrationists*, Hauser's politically tinged satire about a naive American diplomat in a totalitarian state. ("But, above all, Mr. Etheridge -- stay away from the *wives* of the colonels!") Phrases to greet his eye and ease his brow: "Effervescent but provocative. . . . The most fun in many a Broadway season." Or, when particularly at a loss, he could stand at the desk, lean over, and peer down through the window at the empty alleyway below.

On this Monday, however, it was a peculiar and rather insistent noise that distracted him: "Kssh! Kssh! Kssh!" Rolling his eyes, he glanced from the keyboard to the ceiling and waited for silence. Then, appeased, he started typing again. The noise returned: "Kssh! Kssh!

Kssh!" His fingers, usually as fluent as his dialogues, misstruck repeatedly: "*You nwan, of coruse, thaat . . .*" Patiently, he tap-tap-tapped the cursor back to the first mistake. Some of his more ardent admirers would no doubt be surprised to hear that C. K. Hauser *ever* made a mistake. One thing you could be sure of was that in a Hauser play, everything *meshed*, everything *worked*, there were no plot lines left hanging. The playwright meted out the fate each character deserved. Why, he sighed as he corrected the words, couldn't life be a bit more like that? Hauser scanned the monitor and decided that the scene was not, after all, progressing well. It did not happen very often, but there was no doubt this time: He was stuck.

He was still staring at the screen, beginning to lose the meaning of all those elaborate little specks, when his shoulders hunched in a cold shudder. He was being watched. He *knew* it. Abruptly, he poked up his head and glanced around the room.

Of course: There was no one there. He was alone in the house, let alone the room. It was quiet. He listened, but heard nothing. Yet the feeling persisted; the flesh on his back still crawled. Then he got to his feet and, realizing even as he moved how ridiculous he was acting, went to the window and peered out. He did not know what he expected to see -- he was, after all, four stories up, if you counted the sunken alleyway behind the house -- but he saw nothing unusual. There was no window-washer perched on a platform outside his window. There was no beady-eyed carrion bird beyond the glass hovering in mid-air. And yet he could not shake off the feeling that someone was watching him. And for no apparent reason, he had the sense that the secret observer was not friendly in the least. *What* observer? Some imagination! He scanned the alleyway, but again nothing caught his eye.

Shaking his head, he sat down again. He tried to write another few sentences. Then the odd noise came again: "Kssh! Kssh!" It was faint but strangely clear. Could it be from outside, in the alleyway? But he had seen nobody down there. "Kssh! Kssh!"

"Damn it," he muttered, wheeling around in his chair and looking for something to block out the sound. He was *not* going to let some stupid prankster -- if that's who it was -- destroy his concentration. Still mumbling, he hurried from the room and down the stairs to the main bedroom. When he returned, he was wearing a thick black woolen cap and had stuffed some cotton in both ears. *That* should do it. He sat down again and stared hard, almost threateningly, at the computer screen. Then, feeling more than a little ridiculous, he typed a few words.

"Kssh! Kssh!"

Hauser gave another shudder; the sound was faint but clear. All his precautions had done nothing to muffle it. In fact, it seemed as clear as before -- which was, he told himself, impossible. When the sound came again, he got up and leaned over the desk. At first, he could see nothing out of the ordinary. Indeed, the alley seemed to be empty and no peculiar person or object appeared at any of the windows that faced him across the way. Hauser peered at the swaying branches. Who knows, he thought a little confusedly, maybe what he had heard was the call of a woodpecker. But as soon as the peculiar "Kssh! Kssh!" came again, he spotted the little boy standing motionless beside the old scarred trunk of a tree. Hauser blinked in confusion. He could have sworn nothing had been there a second earlier. The boy seemed to be holding his right arm out, almost, it seemed to Hauser, in *his* direction. It took him another moment to conclude that the boy had a toy six-gun in his hand. "Kssh! Kssh!" Hauser stared back at him from his high window. "Damn impertinence!" he thought. "What've I ever done to *him*!" Then, seeing that the boy was content to stand and fire -- in a rather dispirited fashion -- Hauser smiled, shook his head, and returned to the computer.

An idea occurred to him. Since he was increasingly eager to try his hand at something different, he wondered whether it was time to attempt the autobiographical sketches he had planned to produce someday. "Just a few scenes, hardly dignified enough to be called memoirs." He had been asked, two or three times in the past, to write a little bit about himself for the literary journals (once, even, by *The New York Times Book Review*), and the experience had been pleasant enough. He was, it was true, only forty-one, but . . . And since he seemed to be suffering from some kind of writer's block, he could dredge up some incidents from his past -- things that didn't have to be *created*. The boy out there in the back alleyway, all alone with his cowboy pistol, had brought back a few memories. Nodding, Hauser hit the proper keys to begin a new document. "The Adventure of the Blue Suede Shoes," he typed quickly. Yes, that time in fifth or sixth grade when, unaccompanied by his mother, he had gone out one Saturday to the shoe store and returned with the hideous objects of the title. And, despite the recovery of his senses (and aesthetic judgment) the next day, had been forced to wear them to school -- and suffer the implacable judgment of his pals in their high-topped sneakers.

But despite the brittle rustling of his keyboard, despite the ludicrous cap and the cotton, he could still hear the boy in the alley, shooting. It couldn't *be*! Shooting? At him? In his general direction? It was uncanny how the sound penetrated his consciousness (and the other more tangible defenses he had attempted) and diverted attention from his tale-in-the-making. "Kssh! Kssh!" What was the little bastard up to?

When Hauser peered out the window again, the boy was in the exact same position, firing away, as determined but stoop-shouldered as ever. Hauser was too far away to be certain, but he thought an expression of fear flickered across the boy's face. He remembered his feeling of being watched; but he knew at once that this little boy could not be the source of that odd feeling of dread he had experienced. Who *was*, then? Hauser considered shouting out the window, but that was hardly dignified. If only the boy's mother were visible. After looking down at him for another few moments, he decided to confront him in person and explain the need for quiet.

Hauser climbed down the two flights of stairs, went out the front door, and walked down the sloping path around the side of the house to the rear. The breeze was refreshing, but he hardly noticed. A squirrel darted from one limb of a tree to another. Where was the boy? "Typical," he thought. "Waited until he'd dragged me down here, and then bolted!" Hauser was about to leave when the boy stepped into sight from behind a tree. His sudden and noiseless appearance was enough to give Hauser a start.

"Do you live around here?" he said after a moment, affecting a bright conversational tone.

The boy, who looked about seven, seemed to hesitate. Then he shook his head, almost imperceptibly.

"Well, what are you doing, then? Shooting at my window?"

The boy looked down at the pistol in his hand, then back at Hauser. Then he shook his head again.

Hauser frowned. "I *heard* you shooting. That's why I came down here . . . to ask you to stop."

"I wasn't shooting at you," said the boy, not meeting his stare.

His voice was high-pitched but the words were clear.

"So I'm making it up?"

Again the boy glanced at his hand that held the pistol. "Not at *you*," he said finally, risking a peek at Hauser.

"Well, that's where I'm working, that window." He dropped to a squat beside the boy. His clothing seemed oddly old-fashioned: the blue jeans were slightly baggy and were rolled at the cuffs; the shirt was a short-sleeved plaid, something a boy from the suburbs would have worn decades ago; the high-topped sneakers were very plain, just black and white. "So why are you shooting? I don't see any of your buddies around." Then it struck him. Hauser was about to ask him why *he* wasn't in school when the boy shrugged.

"It. I was shooting at it."

"*It*? What do you mean?"

"The thing there. On your wall."

Hauser began to laugh but, seeing the expression on the boy's face, immediately stopped. Something in the boy's solemn, almost resigned manner made his back suddenly chill again with goose flesh, and he glanced over his shoulder at his house. There was, of course, nothing. All he could see was the gray stone exterior, the windows with their curtains and screens, part of the television antenna on the roof (no longer used with the advent of cable). His window in particular -- the one from which he had peered a few minutes earlier -- was innocent. He turned back to the boy. "Do you mean a squirrel?" asked Hauser.

"No," replied the boy. "I know what a *squirrel* looks like."

"You're right. Sorry." Hauser stood up and faced the back of his house again. "But there's nothing there now, is there?" When the boy hesitated, Hauser looked back at him quickly. "Is there?"

"No," came the quiet reply.

"Well, then?" He smiled again. In one of Hauser's plays, the kid would have taken the cue: "Yeah, you're right. Guess I'll mosey along." But this persistent little boy did not budge. "It must have gone away, this . . . thing. Right?" When the boy nodded without enthusiasm, Hauser mussed his hair in farewell. "See you later, okay? Nice meeting you." As he walked away, however, he was thinking, "Strange kid. I'll have to ask Roberta about him."

Upstairs, he had barely begun to type when he heard the first "Kssh! Kssh!" This time, resigned, Hauser switched on the portable tape player on the desk and filled the room with the strains of Grieg's Piano Concerto in A Minor. He was determined to get some mileage, as it were, from his old blue suede shoes, crazy kid or not. And it turned out that he was indeed able to create what struck him as a fairly amusing little sketch about the hapless little Hauser. Yet even as his fingers moved nimbly over the keyboard and the piano cascades spilled forth from the speakers, he could almost swear that he heard the same damn "Kssh! Kssh!" again. Which was, he knew, impossible.

Roberta, back from the office that evening, greeted him with a kiss. "Well, what's that face mean?" she asked with a wry smile. "I did *not* have garlic at lunch."

"No, no." What, after all, was he supposed to say? That he couldn't shake the feeling that someone had been spying on him -- up in his top-floor room? Or that a kid pretending to shoot a six-gun had disrupted his precious routine? "You know the children around here, don't you?"

"Pretty much." "The Millers down the street have a new little

106

girl. . . . I don't think I'd be able to pick *her* out of a police lineup yet."

"Very funny."

"What do you want to know?" she asked, more serious. "Did somebody break a window or something? Or trample the flowers in the back?"

"No, nothing like that. . . . Some kid I'd never seen before was in the back alley. Dressed kinda funny, and seemed to hang around most of the day." He made a grimace. "I didn't get much done. Nothing at all on the new play. A sketch that seemed to be coming along well, but when I reread it, nothing seemed to work. All pretty superficial."

"Good God, you sound like you've been reading that axe-murderer critic from the *Journal* again!"

"Maybe that's who sent the kid." Hauser laughed, then went to the window and looked out. "He's not there now, at any rate."

Roberta raised a brow. "I should hope not. It's probably near dinner-time for him. . . . So what was he doing back there? Setting off firecrackers?"

Hauser found himself growing a little annoyed at her questions. "No. He was shooting."

"*Shooting*? A real gun?"

"No, no," he replied, turning away from the window. How thick could she be? "A toy six-shooter. Nice and shiny, with a fake white bone handle."

"Gee, I haven't seen one of them around in *years*," said Roberta. "All the boys around here have these fancy, modern-looking weapons, from *Star Wars* or whatever."

"He said he was shooting at a thing . . . on the back wall."

Roberta frowned. "A thing? What was it, another of those pesky starlings making a nest in the rain gutter?"

"I . . . don't think so."

"Well?"

"*I* don't know! He didn't tell me, and I didn't see anything."

"He was pulling your leg, Charlie," she said, losing interest.
Hauser gritted his teeth, then immediately stopped. What was getting
into him? He almost never snapped at her like that -- and certainly not
over something so stupid. Roberta moved away, already undoing the top
button of her blouse. "Let me change, honey, and then we'll see what
you've done for supper." She looked back at him, noticing his stillness.
"And why wasn't the little pest in school? Was he old enough?"

"Oh, yeah, I think so. I was about to ask him that myself." In
his mind he was trying to recreate the boy's expression: he seemed
frightened -- terribly frightened -- but determined not to budge.
Something was a bit odd.

Tuesday morning. Hauser stared again at the computer monitor,
turned again to the board with the clippings. He *needed* reassurance.
"An uncanny knack for the satisfying complication." That should help,
he told himself with an ironic smile. But his newest idea, tentatively
called "How Strat-O-Matic Baseball Kept Me From the Neighborhood
Pool Halls," was proceeding laboriously, without the patented Hauser
lightness and wit. Finally, however, after another half-hearted page, he
shut off the computer.

In the silence of the room, it did not take long for the feeling to
begin again -- the feeling of being watched by some malevolent
presence. Suddenly he wished for some noise, some company, even an
Avon saleslady ringing the front bell. Keeping very still, he moved only

his eyes. When they settled on the window, the goose flesh rose again on his back. But there was nothing there! How *could* there be? Then he heard -- he thought he heard -- a soft scraping noise, and he caught his breath. Could it be coming from outside the window? But it was broad daylight, he told himself angrily.

Scarcely conscious of what he was doing, he got up and leaned over the desk to the window. The scraping noise did not come again. After a moment, he slid the sash up and stuck out his head. There was a clear drop to the alleyway -- and nothing else. It seemed as peaceful as ever. He took in the rustling trees, the black pavement of the alley, the tricycle leaning against a fence. Hauser stood still and watched, trying to absorb the calmness, the domesticity, of the scene. Until a loud shattering of glass interrupted his reverie. Hauser twitched in surprise; and as he craned his neck around, trying to figure out where the sound had come from, he thought he heard a burst of laughter. It was a low, ugly laugh. Maybe some punk had broken a window down the street. He waited, still tense. There was no more noise.

As he leaned out the window, he glimpsed a brief movement in the house directly across the way -- where the Nelsons lived, a reasonably amiable couple with a pair of reasonably amiable children. Hauser had quaffed a few beers with them, and Roberta and Maureen occasionally ran errands for each other. His interest quickened: At their kitchen window (it was the back of their house) Maureen Nelson was gesturing animatedly at someone out of sight. Very faintly, muffled by the Nelsons' closed window, he thought he could discern screaming: *her* screaming. Then he caught a glint of a knife: She was waving it wildly. "Hell," muttered Hauser, "what is all *this*?" He looked back at his desk, searching for his smartphone. What if someone had broken into the

Nelsons' house? Oh, God, in *our* neighborhood? Then, as he hesitated, he saw Bill Nelson come into the picture. Why wasn't he at work, as usual? The man wrenched the knife from his wife and flung it away. Then he struck her with the palm of his hand. Hauser felt his face redden in profound embarrassment and distaste: a domestic squabble, turning ugly? Should he call the police? Her shoulders bobbing up and down, Maureen Nelson huddled by the window; but Bill Nelson did not draw near. Hauser waited for almost another minute, then, figuring that the outburst was over, turned away. It would not be up to him to interfere at this point, he decided with some relief. His own window he closed again. Enough of the outside world.

He sat before the blank screen, wondering what to do, feeling fidgety, distracted, even physically uncomfortable in the same loyal chair that had supported him for years. It was still quiet, but he could not help wondering just what other unappetizing scenes were taking place beneath the superficial silence of the neighborhood. The Nelsons! He shook his head. He stared at the blank screen.

It was almost with relief, then, that he heard the familiar sound again: "Kssh! Kssh!" Hauser smiled grimly. At least, he told himself, the kid didn't say "Bang! Bang!" or "Pow!" He waited a moment, then rose and peered out the window. The boy was in the exact same position, directing his puny, imaginary fire at the back wall; he even seemed to be wearing the same clothes. The child's mother should be ashamed, thought Hauser.

"Well! We meet again," he said a few minutes later, squatting down beside the boy. "How are you today?" This did not seem to be a question the boy could answer, and he remained silent. So close to him, Hauser could see the worry if not desperation in his eyes. "Still shooting, huh? . . . At the same thing?"

The boy nodded. There was a slightly familiar look to him that Hauser could not place. The pistol he continued to clasp tightly, almost as if he feared that Hauser would take it from him.

"You know, I don't see anything climbing up my back wall. . . . Do you? I mean, right now? Is it there?"

"No. Not right now," said the boy, almost plaintively. "But it *was*! . . . It's always *somewhere* around."

"What does it do? What does it look like?" Hauser was smiling, but he could not resist a quick glance over his shoulder at the house.

"It's a big thing, all black and hairy. Maybe it's got big teeth . . . and claws."

Hauser pursed his lips. "And it's trying to climb up my wall?"

"No, it's not *trying*," replied the boy at once. "It *is* climbing . . . right up the wall, as good as a spider."

"Maybe it *is* a spider," said Hauser.

The boy allowed himself a smirk. "Are you kidding? It's as big as a tiger or gorilla *any* day!"

"Maybe it's a gorilla, then?"

The boy considered this suggestion for a few moments. "Nah. It's a lot nastier, I think. Real mean."

"So what's this *thing* climbing up my back wall for? *I* certainly don't know it."

The boy hesitated again, then blurted it out: "It's going to kill you. . . . That's why I'm shooting at it." He glanced despairingly at his toy pistol. "But it's so hard with this."

At his words, Hauser had to restrain a shudder. He searched the boy's face for the slightest hint of playfulness. No, the eyes were, if anything, pleading for help, for understanding. Hauser glanced down at the boy's worn sneakers. He forced himself not to look at the back wall. "That looks like a real nice gun there. Can I look at it?"

In response, the boy held it up, but would not let go of it. "I *need* it . . . and you don't believe me."

"Okay," said Hauser with a shrug. "It looks like a Mattel. Do they still make that kind? As nice as anything the Lone Ranger used to have, right?" Hauser doubted that he would recognize the names, but the boy nodded. Hauser saw his eyes flit to the wall. Determined to act as normally as possible, he continued the conversation in a steady tone. "What's your name, by the way?"

"Chuck."

"Chuck, huh?" said Hauser with a laugh. "Well, how about that - - " he began. But he broke off when he saw the boy's eyes flit back to the wall again. Hauser was losing his patience. There seemed to be nothing left to talk about, and he did not want to encourage the boy's fantastic notions about a killer thing. "Well, so long, Chuck. I've got to get back to work." The boy did not answer. When Hauser had walked a few steps, he stopped and turned back, ready to give him some solid fatherly advice. To his surprise, the boy was nowhere to be seen. At once, Hauser felt the hairs on the back of his neck rise. He strode back to the large tree and looked around it. No. "The clever brat," he said finally. He glanced up and down the alley but saw nobody. It was quiet again. Normal. Why, then, did he feel so jumpy?

At the base of the rear wall of his house, he stared up at the window to his study. Because the back alley was sunken to basement level, it meant in effect that his window was four stories up. "No way anyone could climb straight up *that*." And, he added a moment later, there was no damn reason anyone would *try*. Still unable to pull himself away, he continued to look. The wall appeared older than he expected, he thought, and in need of some repairs. Wasn't it typical that they spent their funds and energy on the front of the house while more or less ignoring the back? That crack beginning at the bedroom floor, for example, would need some extensive plastering very soon. There was a long straggly growth of ivy running up the wall, too, and Hauser stared hard at it. Oddly enough, the ivy seemed to have withered noticeably in two or three places, but was somehow green and fresh as it neared the top. Another few feet and it would slip around the gutter and onto the slate roof. Could anyone -- or anything -- use the ivy in climbing the wall? No. It was impossible. It made no sense.

Once again, when he was back in his office, the words seemed very slow in coming. He stared at the screen. Would it make any difference to change the font? Tried something new, just to get started? Then, as he was pondering the relative merits of Helvetica and Lucida Bright, he heard police sirens. Probably a few blocks east of his street and probably at least two patrol cars involved. "Holy cow! What's going on?" He waited patiently until the sirens -- definitely unusual in the neighborhood -- trailed off into the distance. Or what he hoped qualified as distance.

"He was here again today," said Hauser, as Roberta came in shortly after six. "Same gun. Same funny little noise."

"*Little* noise? You seem to be able to hear it pretty well." She removed the jacket of her suit and turned to him with an expression of concern. "And I told you that I'm a bit suspicious of him. Neither Mrs. Kierney or Maureen has any idea who he is. . . . And they haven't seen him," she said after a pause, leading him to glance sharply at her. Just what was she suggesting?

He was wondering whether to tell her what else he had learned. "He says he's shooting at some thing on the wall . . . that's coming to kill me."

Her response was immediate. "What a morbid little creature! And why on earth did he pick *you*?"

"I don't know. I don't know."

"Well, send him on his way if he comes back."

"Oh, I think he will," said Hauser with a wry smile. "Something tells me."

"And did this *something* tell you anything worth writing today?" she asked, in her roundabout fashion touching on an always sensitive subject.

This time, he felt a sharp pang of annoyance at her nosiness. "Not really. It's just not going well." He shrugged and accompanied her into the kitchen. "I don't know," he said, lightening his tone a little, but watching her carefully, "maybe I've just had a boring life."

"C. K. Hauser, the brilliant playwright?" She patted his cheek. "Impossible!"

He smiled back at her. He wanted to feel comforted. She was playing her role as well as he could ask. But something was not working.

"By the way, did you hear about the Pulaskis' car?" she asked, closing the door of the refrigerator.

"No. What?"

"Somebody slashed their tires. All four. Imagine! In *this* neighborhood!"

He could only shake his head. Something was not right.

"Did you bring home the paper?" he asked, not quite sure that he wanted to learn anything more about the world's ills, the world's nastiness.

"Oh, damn. I forgot."

"Don't worry. I can use the exercise."

On his way to the convenience store, however, he came upon a shocking sight: one of pleasant, modest houses had been vandalized. The first-floor windows were shattered, and a couple of swastikas were painted on the walls. Then he noticed the yellow crime-scene tape across the closed front door. He stopped, shaking his head. "What in the world?" After another few moments, he decided not to continue to the store. The hell with the newspaper.

In the middle of the night, Hauser woke from a confusion of dreams, drenched in sweat. Already, the images were fading, the details losing shape, but he vaguely recalled a nerve-wracking pursuit: a lumbering figure that he could never quite shake. Oh, that had happened many times before. And there was something familiar about the figure, as if it were a reminder of much older dreams. Hauser was torn -- trying to remember the thing, trying just as hard to forget he had ever dreamed it. In the end, he lay quietly, staring into the dark ceiling.

Roberta, lying on her side at the other end of the bed, seemed too far away to touch. How could she be so quiet? Why didn't she sense his terror -- no, his uneasiness -- and slide warmly to his side? She looked so comfortable there -- so smug, even. Hauser felt a sudden flame of anger and he had to fight back an urge to reach out and prod her, push her, rouse her, complain to her, wipe that smug expression off her face.

He had to fight it. He saw himself raising his hand, his fist . . . and he barely kept himself from crying out. God, what was happening?

The room was nearly black. Only the windows could be faintly discerned, glazed by oblique moonlight. Hauser tried to lie still for another minute or so, then got up and went to the window that looked out on the rear alley. What would it show him? Oh, but he knew: the same view as always, only from a lower perspective. He hesitated before peering through, listening intently. When he pressed his face to the half-raised glass, he could see only the vaguest outlines of things. Then there was a slight movement. He froze and stared and held his breath until his lungs ached. But it was only a shadow, he told himself finally, only the shadow of the trees across the way, shifting slightly in the breeze, throwing a deeper darkness upon the back wall of his house. Shadows could move that way, couldn't they? That's what it had to be. Hauser took another breath. There was no sign of the boy. He turned away and stumbled back to bed.

Wednesday was rainy, a long dismal gray day punctuated by showers. Hauser, still working slowly and awkwardly, was almost sorry that the weather had changed: now little Chuck would definitely not make an appearance. Not if his mother had a brain in her head. Not if the boy knew what was good for him. As Hauser reread his notes for the third time, there was a sudden gust of wind, and the rain began to rap violently against the windowpane. It was a good day to be inside, he thought, letting his gaze linger on the water-streaked glass.

His smartphone rang, and he recognized Roberta's work number. "Yes, what's up, honey?"

"You're not gonna believe it -- Maureen has left Bill! Turns out he was fooling around, and he would beat her whenever she started to ask questions."

"Unbelievable!" he replied, now regretting that he had not told Roberta what he had seen -- or *thought* he had seen -- the other day. Now, it appeared, Maureen Nelson was staying with her sister a few towns away. "We'll talk later," said Roberta. "Sorry to disturb you. Go back to work!"

So again Hauser faced the computer screen. Why was it so difficult to find the words for the new play? And, even if he had temporarily lost the celebrated Hauser touch, why was it so difficult to turn out a few uncomplicated scenes from his own youth? He typed a few words. How false they looked! And with the news about the Nelsons. . . . Abruptly, the computer gave a peculiar little hiss and the screen went blank. Hell, he thought, now it's problems with the electricity. Muttering, he dragged the old portable typewriter from behind the desk and arranged it in front of him. But when he opened the case and tried the keys, they were stiff, unresponsive to his touch. The keys seemed to move in slow motion, then all at once two or three would strike at the same time -- and stick together near the type guide. He closed up the typewriter and searched for some clean sheets of paper to write on. There had to be *some* around *someplace*. If only he still remembered how to hold a pen. The first sheet he tried to use, however, was quickly smudged by his dirty fingers, inky from prying loose the jammed keys of the typewriter. Burn it, burn them all, burn everything in the room. He sighed, crumpled the paper, and reached for another sheet. So preoccupied was he that it took him several seconds before he heard the familiar "Kssh! Kssh!" from outside.

Hauser sat upright immediately, astounded. How could the boy be downstairs in the back alley in this foul weather? How, indeed, could he *hear* him, today, with the window closed all the way, the rain pouring sibilantly down. With the rain striking the window, he found it very hard to see. For a moment -- an interminable moment in which his heart halted its beating and then reluctantly resumed -- he thought he saw a dark form halfway up the wall. In a peculiar crouch? But his attention had been directed away from his house, to the same scarred trunk of the large tree, and when he looked straight down again he saw nothing. Still, his back tingled. It was the weather, he told himself severely, and a very fertile imagination. But the boy, he saw clearly, was there.

Even through the rain, through the glass, the sound came. To Hauser's ears, it seemed more plaintive than ever. There he was, at the foot of the tree, dressed as before, holding his little arm out. Rain streamed down his face. His sneakers were half-hidden in a puddle. In the twilight of the downpour, the boy's face looked almost ashen.

"What the hell is he doing out there!" The kid had to be an idiot. Or . . . what?

Their eyes seemed to meet. But the boy's pistol, he realized, was directed not at his window but a little lower. It was intolerable. Hauser dashed out of his office and down the stairs and, pelted by rain, made his way around to the back. Even at his violent approach, the boy did not budge. "Kssh! Kssh!" he repeated, his arm, Hauser saw, trembling.

"Give me that!" he shouted, wrenching it from his grasp. Rain was trickling down the back of his collar. And then, as he turned to the house, intending to lead the boy to shelter, he suddenly understood that he was alone. The pistol felt pounds heavier. The rain did not abate, and his high-topped sneakers were sodden. He could barely make out the dark gangling figure on the back wall, its long arm reaching slowly up toward the sill of the top-floor window. "Kssh! Kssh!" said Hauser, as if by ritual, feeling the utter hopelessness of the situation even as he did. "Kssh! Kssh!" But there seemed to be no effect at all. The thing continued to climb, almost to the window now, which had seemed so high, so safe. Then, pausing, it turned its head, and the yellowish eyes sought his through the gray sheets of rain. He knew those eyes, knew the slow toothy smile of that face. Knew it from nightmares long ago, a haunting that had lasted for weeks . . . until he had forced it down. That muzzle, those splayed limbs holding fast to the wet wall. Now, laughing at his impotent little cries, it was circling, retreating from the window, heading nimbly back down. To the ground. To the alley. To him.

If only his aim were truer! "Kssh! Kssh!" Nothing seemed to work. He could almost cry to hear his high-pitched voice. It was down the wall in a moment. Crouching by the side of the house. Then, springing forward, eyes brighter than ever.

"Kssh! Kssh!" he said. But when it was nearly upon him, and its breath burned him, he reared back and flung the pistol into that leering face. Then he was knocked backwards, and his mind went hurtling into a glowing, shifting tunnel of black where dozens of yellow eyes . . .

Hauser awoke with the rain pittering on his face. He was alone. The back of his head ached, and erupted into pain when he rolled over and sat up. For nearly a minute he stayed where he was, resting his forehead in his fingers. Then he looked up at his window, which was a dull gray. There was no light within. Although the rain had slackened, his clothes were soaked. Hauser dragged himself to the front door of his house and staggered inside. Almost six: Roberta would be home any minute. He sat in the living room with a small single lamp on. From where he was, he could see both the front door and the mirror in the hallway. He shivered. He sat quietly, listening to the faint sizzling sound of the rain outside, listening with fascination to the fainter beating of his heart. He was wondering what he could do. He was a shivering thing, a thing without armor. Then Roberta walked in. All at once, she was very loud, saying something about his condition, something that was not clear. She was shocked. "You can't run from it," he was telling her. "You can't kill it." "Kill it? Kill what?" came her voice. "You can't," he repeated, "you can only – " He broke off and tried to shrug. It was all ahead of him, all. And he saw her shaking her head, and in the mirror, as he tried to smile, his eyes gleamed yellow from the lamp.

John Shea

@john.shea.33234

You are invited to the Herland Social Club's

Heritage Weekend

Unfortunately, this is written from memory. If I had all the material I so carefully prepared, this would be a very different story. Entire books full of notes, first-hand descriptions—and pictures! That's the worst loss. We had some bird's eyes—*thanks be to drones*—and, most important of all, pictures of the women themselves.

Nobody will ever believe it probably. Descriptions aren't any good when it comes to women, and I was never good at descriptions anyway. But it's got to be done. The rest of the world needs to know about Herland and the cipher.

It began this way: There were three of us, classmates and comrades—Terry Ho, Jeff Mohani, and myself, Van Jennings. We had known each other for ages, and in spite of our differences, we had a lot in common. Geeks. Terry was born rich and then IPO'd big time just before graduation—next-level encryption software. We never could have done this thing without old Terry. Jeff is a poet, but his parents made him go to medical school. His real interest, though, is what he calls "the wonders of science." I studied sociology, but I've always just expected to work with Terry forever.

This is what you need to know: After the election, the Pantsuiters had enough. They were sick of waiting around for change. In every major city, Herland Social Clubs began popping up. At first, it was a secret hiding in plain sight—their Madewell leather totes monogrammed with HSC just waiting to bid each other welcome. They did everything; they out-trained, out-babysat, out-promoted, and out-cared for each other. Herland Social Clubs came to smaller cities and became powerful in places that used to only see red for miles.

And then, it happened. The Big One. Or, as Jeff, our resident poet, quoted, "One day, the world rent in twain." The earth quaked. El Camino split. Soil turned to liquid and the water just kept coming. Minute upon minute, hour upon hour, it continued. Vancouver, Seattle, Portland, San Francisco, and Los Angeles were simultaneously flooded and on fire. We were surrounded by devastation. It was the noise I'll always remember; the crunching and screaming, the wails of the sirens, and the shattering of glass. The Pacific became a grave. Twenty thousand were dead within the first hours, more missing, never to be recovered, and well over a million instantly displaced.

The cameras on the helicopters and the drones above kept the eyes of the world firmly fixed. But then the screen divided—the President of the United States about to address the nation. Everyone watched as he made his way to the podium, the Vice President beside him. The screens that were still on walls or still in hands showed the President's face alongside live footage of a landslide erasing an elementary school. People gasped. Words weren't possible—*all those children*! The side of the screen that held the President went out of focus and then steadied. "My fellow Americans," he began. He listed the facts: A 9.2 earthquake. A joint rupture, two fault lines, and maybe still a third yet to come. And then, the President of the United States began to quote from the Bible. But he did not quote the verses that many viewers were thinking as they looked upon that landscape. Instead, he began to tell the story of a god overthrowing cities, destroying an entire plain and everything that lived there.

"I knew this would happen," the President said, his finger pointing. "You are being punished." And then the view on the other side of the screen shifted, a world laid to waste. There were still aftershocks rippling. Dense smoke rose and covered the sun as the President began to list outposts. "Don't look back. Flee if you will join us," he said, eyeing the camera hard, his lips tight. "We will take you for the next twenty-four hours, but after that, our borders will close and you will be on your own."

And so, a lot of people left. They made it into Utah, Idaho, and Arizona. They were brought over the Rockies and some were resettled in Raleigh, Austin, and Chicago, locations where the infrastructure was already in place. And then the President and Vice President announced new Silicon Circles in Kansas City, Detroit, Cleveland, and Birmingham—and people were moved there as well. It happened fast because nothing was going across the border into what had once been the West Coast. He built a wall.

I'm still ashamed that we left. We followed a broken I-80 east and made it to Salt Lake just in time. Terry, Jeff, and I were resettled together. We have Terry to thank for that. Otherwise, they never would have put three single guys from the West Coast together.

I knew I'd made a mistake even before we drove through the battalion of tanks and Terry said, "Take off your sweatshirt." At first, I thought he was joking because of the way he was smiling and waving from the driver's seat of his armored 4x4. He'd always been a bit of a survivalist—something we no longer joked about. But then Terry looked back at me through the mirror and said it again. I stared down at my shirt. The Stanford "S" and the towering Redwood met me upside down, reminding me of the land we'd just left behind. You can't imagine looking at Redwoods no longer facing the sky. We left them at every angle—2:00, 4:00, 7:00, done. "You too!" Terry yelled over at Jeff, all while grinning towards the tanks, thumbs up. Jeff was wearing a Google fleece my former girlfriend gave me. "God, we're going to get shot. Don't!" We were afraid to move. Afraid to be seen. Afraid to disappear.

Because, in a way, that's what happened. Everything we once knew disappeared. It didn't fall into the ocean. It was just cut off. We stopped even seeing the pictures. The drones sent out never returned. The satellites were monitored. But that wasn't the real story. The real story was that they all left. In the next few days, the East Coast and Midwest members of Herland Social Clubs left—thousands, tens of thousands, hundreds of thousands—and they took their families with them. The South and The Great Plains left too. They went towards the disaster.

That is how it happened.

Five years passed. And then, I got the invitation.

It was a mistake. It was so *obviously* a mistake. *Van Jennings, you are invited*—there must have been another Van Jennings, I thought to myself, and *she* must have once been a member of the Herland Social Club. But that didn't change the fact that when the invitation arrived with my name on it, I couldn't let it go. And then, there was the problem of the envelope.

"*You are invited to the Herland Social Club's Heritage Weekend,*" Jeff read in awe when I handed him the invitation. "But the HSC no longer exists. I watched a show about it."

I nodded, my hand tight around the envelope. You see, I was holding.

"They all left. They all went…there," Jeff persisted. *There.* Some people tried to call it Herland or Ecotopia or any other phrase they remembered. But mostly people just said *there, here. There.*

In those five years, we'd talked about it in half-phrases, words that probably wouldn't mean much to most people, but I think all three of us missed home. We missed the hazy golden light, the way the fog slipped around the mountains, and our fair city on a hill. Seven hills to be exact. We were nostalgic for the way things used to taste, for places and people we knew. People like us, or at least the people we used to be. The truth is, when you resettle humans, they change. They have to. Adaptation must occur. And I didn't exactly like what we were changing into.

Here's the thing—the invitation didn't just have my name on it. It had our code. The envelope arrived written in our "house code"— Terry's, Jeff's, and mine. It was our joke. We've always used a homebrewed version of a basic pigpen cipher to write messages to each other. Done it for years. V≤□<•■≥<<°⌐⊏◆, or, *Buy Milk, Asshole*. Only someone who knew us would know as much.

And there it was. Our code. Right on the envelope.

"But how did it arrive like that?" Jeff asked.

I shrugged. "It was in the mailbox."

"But how could the mail lady read it?"

"I don't know, Jeff? Maybe she thought, 'I guess I'll just put it in the slot for those Code Guys.'" I noticed that Jeff was looking a little scared. "You know as much as I do, man."

I've always loved ciphers. So has Terry. His company, HoneyPotzSec, isn't just about encryption. It's about a certain kind—the honeypot. Honey encryption isn't new, but we kind of took it to the next level. In lay terms, we produce cipher texts which, when decrypted with an incorrect key as guessed by an attacker, presents a plausible but incorrect password or key. It basically serves up incorrect, yet believable-appearing data to every incorrect guess. So not just a fake, but a believable fake. And they get stuck in it. Thus, the honeypot.

My former girlfriend hated our company logo. Terry *is* kind of a prick—a lovable one, but still. He and Kinsey never got along. Kinsey Wang, the one I can't forget. We all went to college together, but Kinsey didn't leave after the earthquake. She stayed. We broke up seventy-seven days *before* the earthquake. When she didn't answer any of my messages, I assumed she still wasn't speaking to me, and a catastrophic natural disaster wasn't changing anything. The break-up wasn't pretty.

And then we left and there was no way to even send a message.

"I'm still not sure exactly what I did wrong," I said countless times during those seventy-seven days before the earthquake. I also might have mentioned it a few times in the five years since.

"Girl was always lesbian separatist," Terry shook his head. And then, sometimes, after we'd been resettled for awhile, "Move on dot org, mofo. It's overtime."

But I couldn't. I'm not like Terry. In these five years, he's already been engaged multiple times, married once, and now divorced. "Pretty shocked myself that they still want to marry me after they hear about the vasectomy *and* catch a glimpse of the prenup. Must be the charm."

But Jeff understood, so it was Jeff that I showed the invitation to first.

"Shit," he murmured, still staring at the envelope. "They know us?" He sat down, straight to the ground. "But why now?" he whispered.

I sat down beside him. "Some kind of anniversary, I guess."

"What's this?" he asked, holding the parchment up to the light. It was a character, parts curved and others straight. "No," he said the word so slowly. "It can't be—Van, look."

I hadn't noticed before.

"Voynich," I gasped.

"What the fuck you two doing on the floor?" Jeff asked, walking in. "And what about Voynich?" He sat down beside us. The king of HoneyPotzSec, Mr. Encryption. We had to tell him.

All couples have their *things*. Kinsey and I had a few. She bodyhacked, so our junk food was always the night after ending a fast. We'd bone-broth it until about 2:00 pm and then we'd Happy Hour and make out and stop by the store to get everything. *Hardcore Gilmore* was the way Kinsey described our weekend feasting: Sesame noodles, paleo pizza, ice cream, and these boxes of healthy cookies that, no joke, totally tasted like Thin Mints. We'd have sex and watch old *Firefly* episodes, smoke pot, and share sleeve after sleeve of those cookies. And then we'd Voynich.

The Voynich Manuscript is every cipher nerd's windmill. It's our great white whale. It's the apple we can almost taste hanging just out of reach. The Voynich is a 15th century text—carbon dated, o'course—

that is written in a code that, so far, has been unbreakable. Named after the guy, Wilfrid Voynich, who said he found the manuscript basically in a monastery's yard sale. The original used to be kept at the Yale Library—Beinecke MS 408—but after the earthquake it was put in a vault somewhere. Kinsey and I both owned reproductions. You see, the Voynich wasn't just *my* thing—it was *our* thing. Kinsey was into the herbs and the New Age-y bathing too, in addition to the cryptography. Herbs, astronomy, astrology, and bath treatments—that's what the Voynich Manuscript is about. Or that's what we can *assume* the Voynich is about based on the pictures. There are illustrations, lots of them. Alongside and occasionally bleeding into the text are drawings of women bathing in pools of green, alien plants, and doodle-y stars that become flowers. And, on every page, was character after character of a language no one can read or speak.

But they can recognize the text and that is exactly what Jeff, Terry, and I saw on that invitation held up to the light. That character at the bottom of the invitation was *our* character—Kinsey's and mine. The character we believed we'd deciphered years ago. The very same character we'd both tattooed on the inside of our left wrist. A character we believed meant *unify, create, join together, complete*—it was everywhere in the manuscript. But that was the only thing we'd figured out. Before we broke up. Before the world *rent in twain*. Before.

"We're going," Terry decided. "You understand she's baiting us, but let's say they've decrypted it. Shit. We're going."

And so, we went.

"I'm not doing a full-on Scolari," Terry announced before we left.

"What?" Jeff asked for both of us.

"This ain't no *Bosom Buddies* jaunt, my friends. I'm stuffing nothing up in here," Terry said, pounding his chest. Days passed.

"But what *should* we wear?" I asked. Our faces serious.

"Jeans. Tees. Maybe a flannel?" Jeff looked off into the distance. "The magnolias will be blooming."

"If they still have magnolias," Terry answered because I couldn't. My throat caught. We were almost there.

It was Terry's idea to arrive in a hot air balloon. In those years after the earthquake, he'd obviously been lulled into safety, grown nostalgic. As luck would have it, we were caught up in a storm. We almost died, but we went over the coordinates the invitation provided and so we were not rounded up with the rest of the group who arrived for the "Herland Social Club's Heritage Weekend." Caught in the honey, put into the pot. No, unlike the rest of them, we made it over the wall. We were shot at, certainly, and very nearly electrocuted during the storm, but the wind and rain provided force and cover, and we crashed to the ground in the land that used to be known as the Golden State.

If only I had the pictures or my notes or Jeff's or those photos Terry took with his micro-drones, but no—we were relieved of everything. I can tell you this: *There* is something out of a dream. I don't mean "perfect." I mean it is like living inside of an actual dream. A world that is *almost* real but not quite. Both old and new, the barely imagined somehow made logical. But first, we were blindfolded, trussed, drugged, and taken away by high-speed service—you could feel the motion and hear the doors shut and open—and then, we were half-carried and placed onto the ground. When I woke up, my bindings and blindfold were gone, and she was there.

We were in a sunny room, the ceiling full of skylights. There were rugs and cushions and blankets and nothing on the walls. The building appeared to be made of adobe. A large tabby cat stretched awake near my feet. Jeff and Terry were there as well, still blindfolded and trussed. They appeared to be asleep.

Kinsey walked towards me, her face serious.

"You're going back," she said and then kissed me. She'd shaved her head, but that didn't surprise me. She'd shaved it before in high school, and I'd seen those pictures. She smelled the same. She looked stronger.

"No, I'm not," I said. I sounded pissed, but I wasn't. "I came back because of you. Mostly," I said, my throat aching. I looked towards the cat. "I got the invitation."

"We didn't send one."

"I'm not going back," I tried to sound defiant.

"You don't have a choice." She smiled a little and then took a deep breath.

"I never should have left."

"We wanted you to," Kinsey answered, her voice light. "You did exactly what you were supposed to do. You went out and—."

"And what?" I was angry. It made everything worse. "What? Get them to see that robots aren't the new immigrants? Turn the world purple? Teach everybody the proper pronunciation of *pho*?"

"Fuuuuuuck," Terry rumbled from the corner, still bound and blindfolded. "Didn't we get enough of this in college? Has nothing the fuck changed?"

Kinsey nodded towards him and a woman I hadn't seen until that moment walked over to Terry and sprayed something from a bottle at him. He fell back to sleep, his lips parting as he softly snored.

"Please, Kinsey," Jeff said, his voice quiet. "Can't we stay? Couldn't you use us? We have skills. We *belong* here. Please."

She leaned in once again and I thought she was going to kiss me. But instead, she sprayed me in the face and I went back to sleep.

You want to know so many things. You want to know what they wore and grew, how they broke unbreakable codes, how they govern, and if they pray. I will answer everything I can in the enclosed manuscript. I've tried to recreate the notes I made and everything I can remember from the month they let us stay, but I still don't know how to capture the sound of their prayer.

I would ask Jeff, but he's no longer with us. He's still alive! It's just that they let him stay. *There.* Maybe they needed doctors.

When they prayed in a group, en masse, surrounding you, it felt colossal. But when there was only two of you alone, and you listened, it felt built just for you. The day before I was brought back across the wall, we sat in her room together alongside a bed that had been carved by hand. It was really a bench with a mattress.

I didn't know I was leaving.

"Kinda Hobbit," I said, kissing her arm, my nose against the warmth of her skin. She gave me a look. I laughed, "Your bed. Your furniture." And then I noticed the marks in the wood. My fingers went for them. Notches, characters, indentions, images carved from fallen trees. The redwood almost glowed in the sunlight as Kinsey began to pray. When she was done, I opened my eyes.

"Please tell me," I said. Again.

She looked at me and then out the window. She began to sing. She took her time: "*Tell me the stories of Jesus. I love to hear. Things I would ask him to tell me if he were here.*" She stopped for only a second and continued, her voice breaking. "*Scenes by the wayside, tales of the sea, stories of Jesus, tell them to me.*"

I went to church with her family over Christmas once, years ago, back when we were in college. Kinsey wasn't exactly dismissive then, but she never really talked about belief or her spirit before the earthquake. But now—in this new land—they all seemed obsessed with everything mysterious. *Filled with wonder.* They were still scientists, of course. Still engineers and farmers, potters and teachers, but they also prayed and sang and danced nonstop. Mostly in Voynichese, but they no longer called it that.

Someone must have wanted us to discover that they had indeed decoded the Voynich. That they not only read it and could speak it, but they sang it! I begged Kinsey repeatedly to tell me about it, to translate anything for me, but she wouldn't.

"But it's me," I persisted. "You know how much I want to understand."

I stretched out my arms, daring her to match wrists. Character to character, *complete*. But she kept her hands folded and answered once again with excuses, lines from fortune cookies about the importance of mystery and letting things unfold.

"It's only been five years," Kinsey said finally. "It's still too early. For both of us. Be patient."

That set me off. "Maybe I'm a woman now," I said, pissed. Kinsey didn't even look at me so I just kept going. "I'm a woman now because everything I ever loved hates me."

She turned and gave me a smile. "That was good," she said.

"But not enough," I answered.

Jeff understood better than I did. "It's as if they want to learn everything and, finally, nothing is stopping them."

He wrote a poem about the way they prayed, but it was written in the notebooks they took. I can't remember the beginning or the end, but the middle—yes. I've used it as the opening for the enclosed manuscript:

When a world continues, beyond logic, beyond plans, both imagined and known, neither here nor there. Eyes closed, we begin. Eyes open, we—.

It's all I can remember.

Eliza Tudor

www.elizatudor.com
@thatelizatudor

Deer

Julia chooses a seat next to the café door, so she can spot him when he walks in. She's seen his face once, in a picture that Caroline and Mike showed her on Facebook. In the photo he had been wearing a party hat and had a glittery whistle protruding from his mouth. He was pulling an ironically grumpy face, or at least she thought so. He'd just come out of a long term relationship so apparently her friends thought they were a good match. They probably showed him a photo of her as well, otherwise why would he be coming? The single flower on the table shakes as Julia taps her foot against the base.

She picks at her freshly polished nails, the ones she spent two hours yesterday soaking, trimming, cutting the cuticles, filing and buffing and finally coating with three layers of colour. She bites at them now, unable to stop herself. She doesn't want to order without him so she sits at the empty table. She checks her phone. One message from Caroline, Good Luck! with an emoticon of a winky face. She has a feeling that Caroline is putting too much pressure on their meeting, as though she thinks that this will be the beginning of the road that leads to Julia finally getting married at thirty-five. She knows that Caroline thinks she is getting too old to meet someone. Julia puts the phone back in her handbag, the white knitted one that matches her dress.
'Julia?'

A man is standing holding the door open, one foot on the step to the café. She recognises his hair from the photo, although on the screen it had looked like a deliberate bed head.

'Yes, that's me. Hi.'

She wants to stand up to shake his hand but he has already sat down on the seat opposite her, the one closest to the door. She smiles and then stops herself by chewing her lip. She wonders if she's offended him somehow, if maybe he's disappointed in her. She applied her lipstick carefully this morning, first exfoliating her lips with brown sugar, then moisturising with olive oil for ten minutes before applying the coat of colour. She hopes that when she smiles he is looking at her lips.

'Do you still want to go to the lake?' he says whilst chewing the skin on his thumb.

'Sure, I thought we could have a coffee first though? We don't have to.'

He picks up the menu, his coat still on. She notices that his nails are below the natural finger-line, short and jagged, rough at the edges. He looks past the menu at the table shaking, the single flower vibrating its petals. She stops tapping her foot. Puts her hands on the table instead, ignoring the stickiness of the plastic table cloth. She's wearing her favourite summer dress, the one that comes to just above her knees to make her seem free but isn't too revealing. She doesn't care that it's maybe not hot enough yet to wear it.

'Coffee,' he says, and puts the menu flat on the table. 'Black, no sugar.' He looks around the café as though he is looking for someone else. She waits for a moment, to see if he will move, and when he doesn't, she takes her purse to the counter and orders two coffees, one white and one black. The waitress doesn't smile as she serves her. She stares at Julia's nails, the ones that are now pulling away at the cuticle where Julia has bitten too hard. She carries the tray over to the table, two mugs of coffee and a small jug of milk. The cups wobble as she puts it down, a splash of brown liquid resting on top the cloth.

'I said no milk,' he says.

'Oh no, the milk's for me.'

She smiles at him, hoping that he notices her dimples; they're actually scars from falling on a barbed wired fence as a little girl, conveniently placed where dimples would cut into her cheeks. She slides the jug closer to herself.

'So we haven't properly introduced ourselves. I'm Julia. You must be Peter.' She holds out her hand for him to shake.

'Sorry, I thought that was obvious. We've seen pictures of each other, haven't we?'

'Yes, I guess we have.'

She puts both hands in her lap. The posture reminds her of when she would be on her best behaviour at her Grandparents' house, waiting for food to arrive in front of her and the nod from her Mum that she could start eating. She wants to start a new conversation with him, something to make him think that she's interesting, or at least more interesting then he currently does.

'How long have you known Caroline and Mike?' she says.

He wipes a hand down his face like he's wiping off food, the sound of his stubble like sandpaper against his palm. She wonders if it's rude to ask if he's trying to grow a beard.

'A while,' he says.

She takes a sip of her coffee. He hasn't touched his.

'I've known them five years,' she says. 'I used to work with Caroline. She's the one that convinced me to move to Windermere. I've only been here three months.'

He nods.

'How long have you been here?' She smiles as she asks, hoping that he will smile back.

'About the same.'

He reaches out to touch his coffee, taps the side of the mug, then puts his hand flat on the table instead.

'I moved here from Manchester, was living there with my boyfriend,' she continues. 'We'd moved together from London, but I found out he was cheating on me. That's why Caroline and Mike suggested that I move here, for the peace and quiet. It's a charming little village.'

He nods.

'Sorry, that's too much information, isn't it?'

He takes a sip of his coffee, blowing on it first. She takes a gulp of hers, glancing inside the mug at the diminishing liquid.

'Why did you move here?' she asks, looking behind her out the window, a couple walking past with a new born baby in their arms, heads bowed to look at the wiggling figure rather than the pavement.

'Ex-wife,' he says.

'Oh, I'm sorry to hear that.'

'Don't be. She's an idiot.'

She watches him twitch his carefully trimmed moustache. His whole beard black, like his hair, except for the grey above his lip. She's not quite sure how old he is. The sun is hot on her back through the window. She wants to move. She can feel a bit of sweat gathering at the edges of her hair line. She reaches up and wipes it, as subtly as she can.

'You drink your coffee very fast,' he says. He glances at her hand as it wipes the sweat off. She gives him an embarrassed grin, keeping her lips together. Licks her teeth afterwards to check her lipstick.

'Do you like coffee?' he says. 'I prefer tea really but in places like this they never make it right. It's always too strong or too sweet. They never seem to be able to make it the right way.'

It's the most she's heard him say since they've met and she's not sure if he's waiting for a response.

'I like coffee,' she says, finishing the last sip and putting it down on the table, next to the brown puddle that's yet to sink in. She keeps a grip of the mug, stroking the sides as if it's still warm.

'Perhaps we should, when you've finished I mean, we should get going to the lake. It's a lovely day for it,' she says. She points out the window as if he won't quite know what she means if she doesn't show him. She loves the sunshine, something about a sunny day makes her want to be outside all the time, to forget about living in houses or caravans and just sleep under the stars. Though she knows she would hate being outside as soon as it got colder. She's disappointed that he doesn't seem excited about the sun.

'How old are you?' he says, raising his chin towards her.

'You shouldn't ask lady her age,' she laughs, can feel her cheeks heating.

'I've always hated that phrase. So it's okay to ask a man his age?'

'Sorry, it's just a saying. I'm thirty-three, if you really want to know.'

'Oh.'

She wants to ask him back but he seems immediately distracted by something else, swinging back on his chair and looking out of the door.

'Are you looking for something?' she says.

'Just checking on my car.'

She leans back to look out the window, heating up in the sun. Cars are lined along both sides of the street, facing down the hill towards the lake. She tries to pick out which car is his; the polished Land Rover, sticking out too far into the road, the sports car left with its roof off, the BMW? She turns back to the table. He's still looking out.

'So why did you break up?' she says. 'I mean, I know I shouldn't really ask that but we've already shared most of our stories, right? Why not finish them.'

He takes a sip of his coffee, tipping his head back and hanging his mouth open to catch the last dregs.

'I told you. She cheated.'

'I'm so sorry. Did you try and make it work after? Did you forgive her?'

'Why would I try and make it work? She cheated.'

'I was just asking. Me and my boyfriend tried to make it work for a while after. Only made it six months. Perhaps that was stupid? I don't know – do you think so?'

He bites the edge of his thumb, peeling a slice of skin off with his teeth.

'Sorry, I shouldn't have brought it up. Maybe the sun will cheer us up? Shall we?'

She slides her chair back and stands, waiting for him to follow.

'I didn't realise you needed cheering up,' he says. She can't tell if he's being sarcastic or not.

He stands, his chair squeaking against the tiled floor. Nods over to the waitress. He walks out the cafe door before she has a chance to put her denim jacket and carefully picked summer hat on, pulling her dress down over her thighs. She has to walk quickly down the hill to follow him to his car.

In the car they wait for a few moments before they speak; she is worried that he's one of those drivers who can't concentrate on the road and have a conversation at the same time. She tries to look relaxed. Rolls her shoulders back and puts her hands in her lap. She looks out the window. The ten-bed house converted from a bed and breakfasts, no vacancy sign still hanging beside the open balcony window, the woman in the head scarf cleaning inside; the park encircled between the houses and the concrete streets, a single swing untouched, a sea-saw abandoned with one side up; the family walking up the hill towards the park, baby wrapped in pink in her arms and their little boy in front staggering forwards as if he doesn't have possession of his own legs yet. They drive past the houses, the cafes, the walkers, follow the road that curls around the park out to the main road towards the lake. He flicks the radio on.

'You have a nice car...' She glances around, from its sun roof, to its four manual doors, to the rubbish in the back. She notices the fast food packages on the floor then turns back. 'It's very cosy.'

'Did Caroline mention where we were going?' he says.

'She mentioned we both wanted to go to Lake Windemere,' she says. 'That's funny, I've been talking about it for years but Caroline and I have never...'

'Did you bring anything?'

'Anything? Like anything at all?' she scratches her cheek.

'Any food?'

'Food? No, Caroline said it was all organised, that you were bringing everything.'

'That's fine.'

'I'm sorry if...'

'It's fine.'

He has a straight posture at the wheel, his arms are stretched out at full length without a bend in the elbow. Julia remembers how her mum had told her never to sit like that when she was learning to drive; if another car hits you the shock penetrates your arms into your spine and can paralyse you for life. She thinks about telling him this but decides against it.

He reaches up and opens the sunroof, winding the handle round and round to make the glass recede. The car swerves slightly with his movements. She lifts her arm to help him, or to try and take over to stop him swerving but he doesn't let her. Instead, she touches the back of his fingers lightly, remains there for a while, then pulls away.

'I can help with that,' noticing how pleading her voice sounds.

'I can manage.'

The strap of her dress has fallen down her shoulder from lifting her arm. She blushes, bringing her hand back down to correct it. She looks out the window, turning her head far enough so she can't see him out of her peripheral vision, and hopefully all he can see is the back of her head. 'I haven't done this before you know. I don't normally go on dates,' she says.

She swallows. When he doesn't respond she turns to look at him, tries to look at his eyes through the edges of his sunglasses. 'Of course I've been on one or two. But never a blind date. It's usually with someone I've met a few times or spoken online to, you know? Have you?'

'Have I what?'

'Have you dated before?'

'I try not to make a habit of it.'

He leans forward and fiddles with the knob on the radio. Static interrupts music between the channels. He stops on a station that has an over-excited man talking about old time classics. Walking on Sunshine starts to play. She feels relief at how bright the day is, how hot the sun feels on her scalp coming through the sun roof, it calms her nerves a little. He hums to himself, starts to nod his head. She thinks she can see him almost smiling. His finger taps on the steering wheel at something which might almost be a rhythm.

She turns her body towards him, legs resting on the gear stick. 'I love this song,' she says softly. 'It reminds me of my dad.' She doesn't realise how the phrase can be interpreted until she notices his reaction. What she means is, it reminds her of that effortless feeling she used to get, when her dad was cleaning the house, listening to music like this, spinning her around or zapping her with the hoover every now and then, and how it made her feel like anything in the world was possible. She doesn't tell him what she means.

He stops humming and grips his fingers around the steering wheel. She turns to look out the window, adjusting her skirt back over her knee. She chews the ends of her nails, wanting to stop because she can see the gel turning white with her teeth marks, but she can't. She picks at the edges of them, trying to lift the bottoms of the nail up near the cuticle. She doesn't know why she bothered to do them anyway, they never last. After a few moments, she turns to him and asks: 'So what do you do, as a day job?'

'I hate that question.'

'Sorry. What do you like to do in your spare time?'

She feels as though he's rolled his eyes behind his sunglasses. He clicks his tongue, pushing it into the corner of his cheek.

'Well you know, I'm interested in everything. Same as anyone else. I like whiskey I guess. I like reading about the war.'

'Ah, okay.'

She waits for him to return the question. Walking on Sunshine finishes, the chipper DJ's voice breaking through their conversation. He pushes harder on the pedal, the car speeding up and they turn onto the winding road, surrounded by trees with carefully pruned branches. The wind rushing faster through the open windows. She holds her dress at the knees to stop it from blowing up. She tries to talk over the wind, making her mouth wider to be heard but he doesn't respond, or he can't hear. She lets her hair blow over her face, into her eyes, into her mouth, her hands too busy holding the dress down.

It takes them an hour to drive to the entrance of the woods. They'd been told by Caroline and Mike to avoid the main part of the lake, at the bottom of the village where all the tourists go. If they drove around the village to the other side of the lake it will be more peaceful. They'd said that no one went there. There is a path of flattened grass, where locals have been before from the clearing to the edge of the lake, though there isn't an official footpath. Peter parks the car in front of this, the passenger entrance opening directly onto the path. He turns off the car and steps out. The silence seems louder without music and wind. She opens the door herself, carefully balancing her sandals before stepping out. She smooths down her dress.

'It's beautiful,' she calls, as he gathers carrier bags full of food from the boot. He refuses her offer of help to carry them, walks slightly ahead of her the whole way, calling back to her to say that he knows the way. He ignores the colour-coded directions engraved into wooden poles. She follows him, stopping every now and then to shake stones out of her sandals or smooth her dress down. She didn't expect the path to be so bumpy. Her white dress has already caught the dust.

The path leads a short way through trees and arrives at the edge of the lake. From here, they can see the village on the other side, people lying on the banks, trousers rolled up and paddling in the water, children with their brightly-coloured jelly shoes. She holds her hand over her brow to block the sun and looks up to the hill where the cafe is.

'It's beautiful isn't it?' she says. He is laying down a picnic blanket behind her, throwing it up so that it catches the air and pulling it down slowly to earth, repeating it multiple times. She knows better now than to offer to help.

She steps a little further forwards letting the water touch her toes. Over here there's no bank to separate the water and the land, only the water, the waves gently responding to the tourists on the other side of the lake, touching mud, then her feet. Nothing to tell her not to step in further. She bends to take her sandals off.

'You'll get muddy feet,' he says from behind her. He is unpacking the carrier bags and laying out the food as if they're about to feast. It is only eleven thirty. She digs her feet into the mud and lets it seep between her toes, then bends down to wash it before he sees. She realises that her bending over means that he can possibly see her knickers. She smoothes her hand over the back of her dress to check; it feels short but not above her pants. She turns around to see, part of her would like to catch him looking at her, but he's already walking away.

'I just need a piss,' he shouts, barely turning his head. She watches him disappear between the overgrown trees.

'That's fine, I'll wait here,' she shouts, but she hears the insincerity in her own voice.

She sits down on the edge of the blanket, wiggles her toes in the grass and mud, and some grains that might be memories of sand. The earth feels cool against her scorched skin, her legs beginning to prickle from the heat. She looks at the raised veins in her feet where the blood has rushed to the skin's surface to cool her down. It has been a year since someone has touched her skin, someone other than a friend or her family. Since someone has touched it in a way that meant something more than platonic love. It had been a long time since she felt wanted. She thinks, maybe he is okay, he might be shy, and a little weird, but perhaps he just wants someone to want him, like we all do.

She swings her legs and splashes a little water back up her calves. Watches the brown droplets settle and fall. He's been gone a while. She has no watch to check but she feels as though it's been a while. The distance of the laughter and splashes from the other side of the lake make her feel that time is even longer. He's been gone too long. She takes a polystyrene cup that's been carefully laid out on the blanket and fills it with the plastic bottled wine that he's bought. From the way it stains the edges of the white cup she can tell it will stain her teeth and tongue. She takes a gentle sip, letting it sit in her mouth a while before swallowing. It tastes like hangover to her.

She looks back into the woods. The overgrown trees form a wall of leaves and branches, casting a blanket of shadows on the floor. She holds her breath to listen to the birds but hears nothing. Licks her teeth before taking another sip. He's been gone too long. She feels like she should look for him, or at least call out to tell him she is worried. She checks the picnic blanket, his phone and wallet loose on the top. Dusting her feet, she slides her sandals back on and buckles them with wet hands. Folds the edges of the blanket down to cover his belongings. She carries the wine to the entrance of the woods, and then puts it down beside a trunk to pick it up on the way out. She imagines the insects that will be swimming in it when she returns.

Glancing up at the sky she notices that the crystal blue has darkened, clouds are beginning to interrupt in short sharp stops, like floating exclamation marks. It reminds her of the last dinner with her ex-boyfriend, his Mum's starched white table cloth dotted with grey stains as the evening went on, the glass of red wine spilt like the final goodbye to carefully washed linen. She slides her hands down her dress to the edge of her knees, dusting the marks off. Calls out to Peter. He doesn't answer. She strokes her palm around a tree as she made her way inside, past the walls of branches and leaves. Its bark rough, flaking at her touch. Her footsteps seem louder here somehow, they have things to break, twigs and fallen leaves. She walks slowly, glancing in all directions. She doesn't want the embarrassment of catching sight of him pissing.

Even in the shade, the heat makes her sweat. She can feel the edges of her hairline growing moist. Her breath growing heavy. She calls out for him, a little louder this time, annoyed that he's been gone so long. The crunching under her feet reminds her of the walks she used to take with her dog. Their house backed onto the largest woods in the country, and being an only sibling she would get bored of the company of her toys. Instead she would go on day long walks, collecting sticks and leaves, and snails if she could find them. Looking for the muddiest, loneliest corner. She hadn't thought much of it then, but since moving away, she found herself constantly searching for a similar place. A place that felt isolated and good company at the same time.

She looks up. The clouds moving quickly ahead, the trees becoming more spacious. She feels relaxed for the first time today.

Perhaps for the first time in a year. She's comfortable in her clothes, she feels warm, there's a cool breeze every now and then that catches her dress and tickles her thighs. She smiles.

There's a cough from behind her, far enough away that she knows it's not someone watching her. She turns around.

'Peter?'

She looks between the trees.

'Peter?'

'Over here,' he calls.

He's crouched a few feet away from her, resting on the roots of a tree. His head in his hands and something large and dark is on the ground in front of him.

'What is it?' she asks.

When she's closer to him he lifts his head. He doesn't look at her. The deer is lying on the floor in front of him, its body on its side and its head twisted up to face Peter. Its horns rest against the tree. Its eyes are open. Unblinking. She watches them for a while. Peter crouches down. He sniffs. The skin on his cheeks and eyes are blotchy.

'What's going on?' she says.

She steps closer, stands next to the deer's stomach. White spots on the fur. The chest isn't moving. She looks around. She can't see any other people. Peter rubs his eyes and speaks from behind his palms.

'I found it wandering the woods. I was standing a bit back from it, maybe thirty feet or so. I tried to edge closer...' He stops and swallows, wipes his nose on his sleeve. 'I wanted to touch it. I managed to get close. I nearly touched it.'

He looks up at her. His bloodshot eyes embarrass her. She looks down at the deer, smoothing her dress.

'It didn't move. I eventually managed to stand next to it and it let me touch it. It's breath was heavy so I patted it's neck, nose, antlers. It didn't move, Julia. It let out this groan, like, a hangover groan, angry or annoyed or something. And it lay down.' He leans forwards and touches it slightly, as if checking that it's real.

'Deers shouldn't lie on their sides, I read somewhere that once they lie down they can't get up. I pushed on its antlers to try to encourage it to stand. But it didn't. Its breathing slowed, it stopped blinking.'

He looks up at her. She sucks her tongue to the top of her mouth. 'I don't know what happened,' he says. 'I don't know how it died.'

He reaches up to her, strokes the edge of her little finger with his hand, looking back at the deer.
'Look at its eyes, Julia.'

They were solid black, reflecting the branches hanging overhead. She looks closer. She can't see any pupils; she doesn't know if there are supposed to be pupils. He grabs her hand.
'It must have been sick Peter. It's not your fault.'

She's not sure why she said the last part. It had felt right somehow, it had come out naturally, but once she's said it the words feel awkward hanging in the air. She wants to say something else, to replace the words, but can't think of anything else to say. He lets out a small sound. She looks down at him. He's crying; unashamedly, wrinkled chin and wet face. She feels like she should cry too, like maybe that's what he would like, what he's waiting for from her, but she can't force herself to.

She looks behind them, back to the wall of trees where the picnic is waiting. The light seems to zig-zag where they are, where the tops of the trees are breaking open. There are cracks of dirt around them where the roots are growing too big for the ground. She nudges her toes against a fallen leaf, gently crushing it. She wants to wiggle her fingers.

'It's okay Peter,' she says, though she can't think of anything more to say.

He lets go of her hand and grips her leg, wrapping his fingers around her calf. He rests his head on her knee. His crying is making him shake. She can feel the wet of his tears against her skin. The stubble on his face against her freshly shaven legs. She holds her own hands to her chest, out of the way of his. Picks at her nails.

She looks around the woods, looks behind them, looks at the deer and the dirt on the floor. The cracks in the ground. She looks anywhere else but at him.

Nici West

www.lostforwordscopywriting.com

@NiciCopywriter

Much Rabbits

Andy Rintala and I were friends as kids, but when my mother insisted we attend the Catholic church instead of the Lutheran church at the top of Bridge Street like all the harbor Finns, we drifted apart. He never made fun of me like the others in high school, but the fact he ignored me hurt worse than if he had. When he walked into my office, I had a hard time recognizing him. I'd never made a class reunion, so I wasn't prepared for the thinning hair and jowls or the middle-aged paunch. Maybe I frowned without realizing it because his expression changed when our eyes locked.

"Raimo, long time no see," he said. Only my family ever called me *Raimo*. Outside the house, I was Ray or Raymond just as I knew his real name was *Antero*, Finnish for *Andrew*. My brother, the high school jock and prom king, was *Riekoriki* on the birth certificate, but I never heard my mother use anything but her pet name for him, "Rikki," except the one time she was furious with him because he hadn't saved me from the burning tent that disfigured my face when I was ten years old. He was *Rick Jarvi* on every one of his dozen sports trophies. His friends, even people he didn't know, called him "Twenty-Two" for his jersey number.

I gestured for Andy to take the captain's chair from the *Orion*, a lakeboat destined for scrap docked in the harbor when my brother and his friends looted the pilot house one night of whatever they could haul away. Rick wanted the chadburn. He knew somebody named Chick who said he'd pay a hundred dollars for it. That old chair had been stored in my family's garage for twenty years before I came across it.

We shook hands. "Yes, a long time," I said.

Maybe seeing me after so many years reminded him of our high school days, but whatever the memory, he seemed embarrassed.

"How's Rick? I heard he was living in California," Andy said.

"No, he's been home for a while," I said.

I didn't elaborate. It was complicated. I'm a patient listener as a rule; it helps if you're in a people business. Maybe the rancor of his teenaged betrayal made me cut through the small talk.

"What brings you here?"

"Mike. You know Mike? My son Mike," he said. "He's missing. He hasn't called for ten days. Nina and I, we thought maybe you could—you know, look into this for us. We heard you was in this business."

This business. . . The lurid connotations of my profession rearing its ugly head again. The elegant script of *Ray Jarvi, Private Investigations* scrolled across my plate glass window notwithstanding.

"When was Mikko's last contact with you?"

Using Mike's family name reassured him like a salve. He talked for the next twenty minutes while I interjected a question here and there.

"You said Mike's cell phone went to voicemail the first time you called and then it went dead. But did he leave a name, a number, write anything down?"

"Just this," Andy replied. He handed me a small, tightly folded piece of paper; it reminded me of the "kites" convicts shoot along their cell corridors with a long piece of string.

"It was on the fridge, stuck to a magnet," Rintala said.

Just a woman's name: *Ariana Lantana*. It sounded like the name of a cartoon.

He filled out my one-page contract for hiring my services, which surprised him a little, as I think he expected a discount, one Finn helping another. We shook hands again at the door. He reminded me of my father, and I wondered if worried fathers all walked like that.

I'm not superstitious. I had that burned out of me along with the skin I'd lost or sometime during those years of skin-graft operations. The long-haired drunk in his black vest happened to pass my window just as Rintala left. I watched him shield his eyes from the glare while he stuck his face right up to the glass like some nosy kid. After a moment of this ritual staring inside, he strolled off. It irked me that I'd even think of taking an old wreck like him for an omen.

I got to work. I was fortunate that Mike belonged to a generation that loved to put everything online. His *Facebook* page gave me the goings-on of his recent life, which his father had roughly outlined for me earlier. Mike's divorce was a bad one; Judy had primary custody of the twins, a pair of smiling towheads. Judy was cropped out of the photos. Andy left the reason for the split vague: "High school romances, they never last" was his judgment. Mike's last updates hinted at a new romantic interest, although no one was named, and nothing was added after his last posting of a selfie he'd taken ten days before he disappeared from Northtown.

I'm compelled to tell prospective clients looking for missing loved one to talk to police instead; their resources are superior, and their access to credit-card information makes me weep with envy. My databases are good, and I can get BMV access, and I learned early on that public records you can google are full of inaccuracies; however, thanks to the lawsuit after my accident, I have the financial means to afford some of the best databases private investigators, process servers, and repo professionals go to like *Skip Smasher, Skip Max,* and *IRBsearch.*

Maybe I'll be lucky, I thought. *Maybe this Ariana is the cause of Mike's disappearance and that'll simplify things.*

Only TV gumshoes do deep dives. Mike had no criminal past or owned property other than his house on Gulfview, now his ex-wife's residence, and you can't get account-specific records of a person's finances or phone records unless you think going to prison for third-party violations of the Gramm-Leach-Bliley Act is a good thing. Andy said he threw out the last phone bill, but he told me Mike must have made a call from the house while his own phone was recharging.

I called Judy, who'd graduated from Sts. Stephen and Basil the year after Mike's class. She didn't sound overjoyed to hear from me.

The house was a remodeled Victorian. The marble mosaic in the foyer reminded me of one of Mike's *Facebook* photos where he'd displayed the honed floor tile mosaic he'd crafted; it was a winter scene of a boy on a toboggan careening down a hill. From the nearby forest, a wolf with yellow eyes looked out.

I left my shoes on the runner. "He did a great job on that medallion," I said.

Judy made a face. "He brags about it enough on *Facebook*."

We were sitting on blonde wood stools in the kitchen. She set a cup of coffee in front of me on the granite countertop.

"Beautiful house," I said.

"My consolation prize," she said. "Look, Ray, I don't mean to be rude, but I don't have any information for you. His old man is driving me crazy every day, asking if Mike has called yet."

"Is it like Mikko to just up and go? No word to you about where he's going or when he might be back?"

"Ha, his dad still calls him that," she said. "He made his father call him 'Mike' around the kids."

"From his postings, I gather he has visitation privileges."

"Every other weekend," Judy said. "My God, I wish he'd stop with that! Telling the whole world everything about us, his family, his marriage, how much he loves his kids. It's sickening."

After I sobered up years ago, I read a lot of Russian novels. I remembered a passage from *Crime and Punishment*: Razumikin lamenting after a drunken episode how he had poured out his heart to Dunya, a girl he'd just met. . . *all the sordid catastrophes of my heart*. . . the line struck a chord in me somehow.

"Wouldn't he have called if he couldn't make it?"

"I couldn't deny him that. Seeing his kids, you know. But him and that damn lawyer pushed my buttons. He's the one who cheated, not me. Why should I care who he's seeing or where he goes?"

"Does the name 'Ariana' mean anything to you?"

"No. If it's one of his online whores, I don't recall it."

"Lantana?"

"No. It sounds like a flower."

"It is," I said. "It's also a city in Florida. Did Mike ever mention going to Florida?"

"No."

The rest of our conversation went like that. I left her standing in the foyer, a beautiful woman in dishabille, blonde hair tied off in a practical ponytail, and had a flashback of her in the paper years ago smiling, surrounded by her homecoming court. The scowls she exhibited were Mike's legacy. His online photos showed a confident man, handsome and fit, the hairline just beginning to recede like his father's. Being scarred has one advantage: you never lament aging because you never had pretty plumage once.

Back in the office, I called my friend Bart in the sheriff's department and told him what I needed.

"You might wind up with me as your partner sooner than you think, Raymond, if the sheriff finds out. You know he hates me."

Private investigators don't have access to certain databases law enforcement does. He left a brief message with some phone numbers on my answering machine that night.

The next morning, before dialing, I checked the prefix of a number Mike had called three times the week before he vanished: Palm Beach County.

That struck a chord, a faint bell in the back of my memory. I dialed the number and a voice said, "Pelican Motel." I asked where it was located and was told Weston, Florida.

Across the street from my office on the corner of Bridge and Hulbert was a shop that sold scuba gear, wind-, and kitesurfing boards. It used to be owned by red-haired woman who operated a small business that sold paperbacks and turquoise jewelry. The Navajo Bookstore was one of the few places I didn't feel that familiar tightening in my stomach whenever I enter a public place. I bought dozens of dogeared guidebooks for places I'd never travel to. This was years before I opened my office and not long after I pulled myself out of the drunken, solitary life I'd condemned myself to in self-pity.

The *Fodor*'s guide to South Florida noted this for Lantana, Florida: ". . . an extremely uninteresting city that claims more Finns than most anywhere in the U.S." It goes on to say that the *National Enquirer*, headquartered there, sponsors the world's largest Christmas tree in front of its offices, "a focal point of great interest each year," according to that description for 1988.

The part about the Finns is still true. I googled it. But the headquarters of the *Enquirer* moved south to Boca Raton that same year and ended the annual Christmas tree event.

I had this much from the note on Mike's refrigerator: Lantana wasn't a surname; it was the city in Florida where Mike had gone to meet a girl named Ariana.

* * *

The Pelican Motel clerk was an Hispanic male in his twenties with acne-scarred cheeks. He was helpful—brothers under the skin, I reckoned. He told me Mike had checked in under his own name two days after he left Northtown, paid in cash, and stayed one night. For a twenty, he gave me the name of the maid who cleaned the room he stayed in. She was due in at 4:00. I bought an egg sandwich and a Cherokee Red soda and went back to my rental to wait.

Abryanna Soledad was a forty-year-old woman who stared at me longer than most who, when they realize they're staring, cut their eyes away and don't look at my face again. She seemed unsure, even when I pressed her to take the twenty "for cooperation in a missing person's case." TV cops badge people and get immediate results. My Ohio private investigator license rarely has that effect. She didn't recall Mike from the photo I showed her, claimed she didn't remember anything unusual about the room he stayed in during that week. She did remember a young woman who stayed there around that time because she had two boys who visited the room. Because they left the room a filthy mess, *un lío, desastre*, she said and scowled at the memory.

The clerk, whose name was Trujillo, told me the girl signed herself in as Renata DuMaine from New Orleans, had ID for a 21-year-old but, he said, "No way, man. She looks sixteen."

"Looks?"

"She stays here—oh, maybe once a month, like."

He showed me her signature in the book—big loopy curlicues, the *i* dotted with a circle, the tail of the *e* swung back to the tip of the florid *M*, an ego trip.

"There's no license plate number here," I said.

"No, man, she, like, gets dropped off."

Trujillo didn't remember the vehicles she arrived in. In so many words, he made it clear the motel was a trysting place for cheating spouses along the busy I 95 corridor. With all the phony "Smiths" and "Joneses" he must have dealt with, no one named Ariana had ever signed in.

Something about the girlish handwriting, the phonetically similar name of the motel maid's name to Ariana, the childish name on the paper on Mike's refrigerator bothered me. Judy had referred to his "online whores," a bitter wife's recrimination, but it didn't seem much of a stretch to assume Mike had been lured to Florida by a woman. Like his father, Mike was extremely proud of his Finnish heritage, and if a woman he'd met online had intentions of playing him for money or love, whether "phishing" or "catfishing," he'd be receptive to that chord struck, and what's a better gambit than Lantana's dense Finn population to pique his interest?

The teenaged girl was a wrong note, however, and I had no reason to assume there was a connection between Mike's one-night stay at the Pelican and this Renata DuMaine and the cluttered room she and her friends left behind.

I spent a miserable week almost living in the Toyota, shirt stuck to my back, fighting interstate traffic, blinded from windshield glare, the jungle humidity so thick the sweat beads popped out on my forearms seconds after I left the car to walk into the nearest air-conditioned establishment to make my enquiries. The morning heat of Florida sunshine started to depress me as much as a gray November day back home. Only the snowbirds from up North come down here to get blistered and tanned like shoe leather. The locals sneer, take their money, and remain as pasty-faced as lepers. I began to yearn for those pewter skies of home. Every day the sky was scrubbed clean of clouds but by early afternoon, massive thunderheads began to loom overhead as if a judgment from God, and the skies would burst.

Between Weston and Lantana, I hit a fair random sampling of roadside diners, motels, fast-food franchises, and struck out. No one recognized Mike from the photo and no one alerted to my description of a teenager named Renata.

On that Sunday after yet abortive trip with nothing learned, I pulled into the Pelican's gravel lot. I had to call Andy for permission to continue the case. My time, not to mention the accumulated mileage, was getting expensive.

By this time, Trujillo the clerk and I were friendly. He'd wave as I came and went. I had a hundred-dollar bill folded inside my wallet for him when I had to leave for him to call my number in Ohio if or when this Renata showed up again.

The sun was at the right angle, when I turned toward my end of the L-shaped motel because I could see him clearly through the glass. He was with a customer; he looked up when he heard the gravel crunch under the chassis of my car as I passed. The nod of his head said it better than words: *She's right here—*

Renata DuMaine in the flesh—signing in.

I held my breath and pulled up to my room, my heart thudding with thanks. Sometimes the gods give us these little gifts. . .

She headed to a room midway down. I keep binoculars in a backpack on the seat, but I had a good look at her. She looked sixteen, seventeen, stringy, dirty blonde hair, black tee, cut-off Levi's and sandals, a tattoo on her right ankle I couldn't make it out but the one on the inside of her left wrist was clear and slanted in Chopin script. *Renata* was done in the font style identical to my office window's lettering. The capital *R* expressed with delicate filaments bursting from the petals of a flower.

Tempting to confront her as it was, I decided to wait, so I set up surveillance in the parking lot.

An hour later, a beat-up Silverado sporting patches of Bondo putty like mange pulled into the lot and two teenaged males, one black, one white, got out and went to her door. The black male had his hair braided in dreadlocks and was talking on his cell phone. The white boy was smaller, wore a wifebeater that exposed muscular arms—not buffed like a weightlifter's but rangy like a farmer's—with a tattoo sleeve on the right arm from bicep to wrist, his Levi's were full of holes that looked more wear-and-tear than designer. His Doc Martens were scuffed and the red laces partially undone.

I kept vigil and watched her room. No one left, but cars began arriving, many of them in high-end SUVs. I saw several couples, a few intoxicated, women in club dress giggling, heading for the rooms on either side. I was used to the noise by now—the moans from the vents, the occasional thump of a headboard against a wall. The night air of Florida wasn't perfumed with scents of mimosa and jasmine as I'd expected; instead, it reeked of diesel fuel and something that stung my nose like burnt sugar. Feral cats prowled at night, their eyes lit to incandescence by the cars and semis pulling in for the night. Somewhere behind the motel, the jarring cries of a lone female cat in heat set my teeth on edge.

I went to my room, collapsed on the bed, and put the pillow over my ears. The whole world was a scene out of Bosch painting. I told myself I was clueless and going nowhere. In the morning, I intended to leave.

When I stepped out a little after dawn, go-bag in hand, I felt the humidity revving up. The sun had already painted the vegetation across the street and limned the kudzu vine strangling a transformer and crawling down the telephone wires. A tribunal of pigeons sat up there as if to judge my failure.

She walked right into me as I turned the corner on my way to the lobby. I don't know what it was. Before this, I was a private eye in name only. I used the phone and the computer for the few cases I had; here I was in Florida, on a case that required me to do something, anything, and I had failed. I had nothing to lose.

She apologized for bumping into me and started to move around me. She looked the same except for the mussed hair and her body gave off a warm smell, not stale like day-old perfume, but a slightly rancid scent.

"I'm looking for this man," I said.

I held the photo out and watched her face. Her eyes lit with recognition, no doubt about it. Then her gaze shifted from the photo to my face and she flinched. Maybe my scars disoriented her, caught her off guard, but she had hesitated too long.

Before she could recover, I moved into her space a little more, forcing her to step back and threw the dice: "He came down here a couple weeks ago to meet Ariana. Where's Ariana?"

If I'd asked for Mike, she'd probably have trotted out a quick lie and gone her way. The gamble worked. I followed it up before she could get her bearings.

"You're Ariana's friend," I said. "Mike told me about you. Nice to meet you. . ."

"I'm—I'm her sister," she said finally.

"That's right, I forgot. He said he was meeting Ariana's sister, but I forgot your name."

"It's Renata," she said.

The adrenalin rush was giving me tunnel vision. I made the conversation sound as nonchalant as possible. She had all the marks of a street-smart runaway and, my luck, I'd gleaned just enough experience on the job to recognize the shiftiness, the body language, the amoral ease of practiced liars and street hustlers like her.

I had her at ease—even made a joke about my "scary face" and catching her off-guard. She was mentally shifting gears, talking to me about her "sister" and how she and Mike met online and were "dating pretty heavy." I didn't probe. I was sure she was sounding me out. I kept up the inane chatter about starting over, the heat, the cold of Northern Ohio, to keep her off-balance.

"Look, I'm passing through, just on my way to Key West. Mike emailed me, said to drop off his share because he'd met your sister down here."

"What share?"

"We had a small paving business, sidewalks, driveways, that kind of thing. It folded."

"You married?"

"With this face, are you kidding?" I laughed.

You married. . . Bingo. A man with no family, no one to come looking for him. I felt a lump of ice drop into my stomach.

I prattled on about "leaving it all behind, striking out for new horizons," every dumb cliché that popped into my head hoping I didn't sound like Captain Obvious. Then I took a big chance. If she was anything like the runaways I'd encountered, she'd be a doper. With luck, the serious kind that would knock their grandmothers over if they saw them standing on a dime.

"It's all the money I owe him," I said.

I flipped open my wallet and showed her the cash I'd brought down with me. It wasn't that impressive, but cash is more useful than a credit card when you're buying information.

"I've got three thousand back in the room, but I don't like to walk around with it. Hell, you never know, right?"

She said she'd take me to her sister's house. It wasn't far, she said.

"Ya'll know where Deem City is?"

I laughed. "No, I've never been farther south than the Ohio River. Never coming back to this place, that's for sure. I'm half-bit to death from bed bugs and those damn cats don't stop howling, not to mention all the mattress-bumping—"

"Them ain't bed bugs, man. Them's chiggers. Look here."

She did a graceful pirouette. "Check out my ankles."

A bracelet of tiny red dots surrounded both legs.

"Renata, how about if I drive you, we go get breakfast

somewhere nice?"

"I ain't getting in a car with a stranger even though you seem like a nice guy."

"Of course," I said, "Sure. Things today, the way they are, you just can't trust people."

"I'm staying with a couple friends," she said. "They'll drive me. You can follow. I ain't ready to go right now—"

"No problem. Here's a couple twenties from Mike's stash. Let's let old Mike buy you and your friends breakfast, and I'll meet you in the parking lot out there—say, about nine? That OK?"

I'd overdone the helpful sucker bit, if my knotted stomach meant anything, but she gave me one last look, her dark eyes boring through me tracking the livid scars on the left side of my face as if they led to an answer. I watched her walk back to her room.

I had time to flesh out the story, and I thought about my gun back in a desk drawer in Ohio. The two boys came out first, Renata trailing behind like a tagalong sister. Jay, the white youth, had a missing front tooth and one of those high-and-tight buzz cuts. They wore the same clothing as yesterday except that Jay's boots were laced to the top eyelet. Jay grilled me, none too subtly. He was the alpha male.

"How'd you get them scars on your face?"

"A bottle rocket fell on the tent I was sleeping in," I said. "I didn't get out in time."

"Man, your face looks like an asshole casserole."

"Gee, really? I wasn't aware of that."

"You bein' smart with me?"

Get back in role, idiot, I ordered myself. *The job, the job. . .*

I said some things about my looks that others had said to me, things that scored channels in my psyche when I was young. It took years for me to accommodate so that I could live in the world without my scars doing that for me.

"You ride with him, Tru," the white kid said.

The four of us walked toward our vehicles. My stomach, already queasy and fueled on nothing but vending machine coffee, roiled as a thick, sweet odor in the rising heat tripped something in me far back in the old brain, the limbic or the lizard brain where we carry our deepest habits.

"I smell something," I said.

Renata laughed. "Take a look in the truck."

In the bed lay three bundles of brown fur knotted by twine around the legs to a long pole.

"Them's muck rabbits," Renata said. "Jay and Tru hunt 'em in the wildlife refuge in Lakahatchee. It ain't legal but they do it anyway."

I saw a couple small wooden bats next to the dead rabbits. I recognized them as fish bats.

"What do you do with them?" I asked her.

"Jay and Tru, they sell 'em to restaurants," she replied. "Muck rabbits in bacon fat. I could go for some rabbit stew right now."

Jay and Tru laughed. It sounded like *double entendre*, and I was the butt of the joke.

"Four dollars apiece," Jay said to me. "Speaking of money, I need money for gas, man."

I gave him twenty and left the wallet open for him to take a good look.

On the way out of the lot, I tried small talk on Tru. Except for telling me his real name was Trumaine and demanding I "crank up the got-damn A/C, yo," I got nowhere. He put his ear buds in and rocked to his music. The rhythmic pounding of rap from some artist spilled from his earholes like slopped milk and filled the car with some of the ugliest words in the English language, mainly *fuck* and *kill*.

I stayed behind the Silverado. Renata's hair whipped about her head; she'd occasionally look back at us, and I could see her well enough to catch a smile or her mouth moving. Her animation in the front seat was owing to the radio's music, I guessed, while Jay's head never moved despite Renata's playfully lowering her head to his crotch a couple times, giving me a show—or else, I wondered, if the new adventure we were on was acting as an aphrodisiac for her.

We were leaving civilization behind: wide open vistas, flatland, tall sawgrass. The deep culverts alongside the road were dried and thick with muck.

I wondered if alligators and water moccasins were slithering around out there. I'd googled Deem City from the motel. A ghost town, *Wikipedia* said. A desolate tangle of vines and abandoned houses, an abandoned sugar mill, *nothing to see here, folks...*

I'm a city boy, small town born and bred. Big cities don't frighten me. Nature does. The jungle especially—all that eating, sex, and death out there. I knew I'd never see a parrot in the wild, unless it was smuggled up from Mexico, or even a canary, unless one got loose. A parrot has other enemies besides man; weasels, for example, like to jump on a parrot's back and go for a ride over the canopy. But the weasel's not using the parrot the way we use Uber. It's waiting for the bird to tire and land so that it can eat it.

Jay left the highway for a dirt road. The Toyota bumped along the ruts behind the truck for miles, slewing in the soft ground. Tru stirred long enough to shout, "Watch it!" when I almost got stuck. The track narrowed to dirt-bike width. Despite the air-conditioning, the smell of swamp rot seeped through the cracks and made my nose itch.

A cement-block structure with flaking, olive-green paint loomed through the underbrush. I saw the Silverado parked near it.

"We're here," Tru said. "Get out."

Jay and Renata walked toward us. Tru was a couple steps behind me.

"Used to be alligators here," he said, pointing to the building. I could make out the faded yellow letters running the length of the building: ALLIGATOR FARM. To my Midwestern sensibilities, that was an oxymoron.

"Show you something," Jay said. His clipped English was a sign of his confidence.

I followed him to the edge of a ravine. The pungent smell of dead rabbits was magnified a hundred times as we approached the edge.

"Check it out," Jay said.

My mind couldn't process what I beheld at first. It resembled a moose carcass—*how ridiculous*—a tangled mass of limbs sticking up, white bone evident in places, bloated intestines seething with maggots. A twig cracking under foot caused a shadowy mass of flies to boil up in a dense column and evaporate before re-forming in midair and settling back to the feast.

"What—what is it?"

"It's your fuckin' friend you was lookin' for," Jay said.

I twisted away at the right moment. The bat Tru brought down was aimed for my head but missed and slammed into my shoulder, shattering the clavicle. I went face first over the edge and rolled into the putrid mess below.

"He ain't dead," Tru said above me.

"Fuck me," Jay's voice. "I got to go down there in that shit and cut him now, you motherfucker."

I rolled away, nearly fainting from the sharp pain radiating like a lightning bolt between my brain and my broken collarbone. Somehow, crazed by fear and whatever enzyme my brain was squirting to get me out of there, was propelling me down that culvert at breakneck speed. Branches whipped my face opening cuts and lashing one eye shut—but I stumbled on, flailing my arms to push aside the branches and weeds. It was a like being inside a dream where you run but your feet are caught in mud or wet cement. But I never stopped moving except for a couple of times when stomach spasms forced me to retch out the coffee I'd drunk and later, a ropy string of yellow bile. I remember stumbling over a wooden trestle bridge, and I remember crossing a half-dozen ditches, wading through slimy, algae-covered drainage canals, and one I had to float across on my back, gulping brown water, my bad arm dangling like alligator bait all the way. I was reduced to one thought: *keep the sun over the bad shoulder* all that long afternoon march to avoid walking in circles.

The thought of Jay coming up behind me with that knife terrified me every step of the way even when I should have realized he wasn't there. At one point, I was delirious, and I snapped to hearing myself talking to Mike, telling him we had to keep moving—*never mind the biting rats*, I said—but the pain was so fierce I sat down and passed out.

By the time I made it to an asphalt highway, it was night. The blackness will stay with me forever. The ceaseless dinning of insects all around me, large bugs hitting me as I stepped, toddler time, one baby step in front of the other, darkness so thick and black I could feel it on my sunburned face, my clothes were shredded to rags, and my pants were caked in swamp muck. I was crisscrossed with deep slashes front and back as if I'd been flogged by a cat-o'-nine-tails. The mosquitoes had dined on me the whole way and I didn't mind. *Better them than cadaver flies*, I told myself.

A truck driver carrying drums of steel coil on Highway 27 nearly killed me and then he saved me. His headlights blew me up in a swath of bright light from my feet to my torso and then my whole body. By that time, the ear-splitting scream of air brakes told me he hadn't seen me until the last second before he slammed on the brakes. He helped me into his semi, wrinkling his nose at the foul smell I gave off. I think I was coherent, although I learned much later from the sheriff's detectives, I was half-in, half-out according to the driver.

Renata (real name Brandi Lynne Sampson, 17, from Lake Worth), Jay (Randall Jay Clemenci, 17, runaway from Broward County foster care), and Tru (Trumaine Hickson, 16, last known address a juvenile detention center in Volusia) were all picked up at the Pelican a day later. They hadn't even tried to run away but they sold my rental to a chop shop in Davie.

On a laptop in the room, a forensics officer discovered ongoing communications from a half-dozen dating sites. The three youths had some of the men they contacted pretty far along in "the grooming process," as he described it to me the day after I came out of surgery. "Your man Rintala was one of three bodies in that tangled, foul-smelling stew we discovered in Deem City," he told me. The other two, he said, were too far along in decomp to make an easy identification.

"They might not be all of it," he said; "one of our search teams found a femur about a hundred yards from that alligator farm structure. We found Army cots inside. Stacks of video games and a PlayStation Four, burner phones and some other electronics boosted from Walmart. They were squatting there when they didn't have cash for a motel."

Mike had been trolling for dates in a site called *Plenty of Fish in the Sea*. The officer brought me copies of the exchanges between Mike and "Ariana."

The news of the bodies had made the Miami stations already. The cop told me there were vans with aerial whips and news channel logos outside the hospital waiting for a word from me. I'd been misidentified as a "victim."

"Who wrote the emails?" I asked the lead detective.

"The kids did," the detective replied. "They're cooperating so far. They took turns coming up with stuff to write. Mostly, we think the girl. The one kid, Randall, he don't have enough brains to pour piss out of a boot with the directions on the heel."

I found it hard to believe that three teenagers could deceive so many grown men. It was more than technology. "Mike wasn't the type," I told the cop.

"Nobody thinks they are until it happens to them."

I had the afternoon to think about it. In Mike's case, I could see how shrewd the messages were. They'd take something he said and feed it back to him as this phantom Arianna. He'd fill it in, coloring "her" in such a way she became an object of desire. They set the hook with Mike's heritage just as I thought. She was Arianna Karhu, a common word in Finn that means "bear." To the other males, a different surname, always feeding them the image they wanted to see in a desirable woman—never needy, always the opposite of the women they'd known or had bad experiences with. Just teenagers. . . with a single G.E.D. diploma among them, yet when it came to fleecing grown men, some professionals, they pulled it off behind the anonymity of a keyboard.

I despised myself for admiring the cleverness of the lures they set. Even the misspellings and wrong word choices were made to service and flatter that male's ego and push him a little further reach time into believing he had the girl of his dreams at the other end of their connection in cyberspace. Even the photos the three used, stolen and photoshopped from various internet modeling sites, many Russian, were selected with the right male in mind. In the cold light of my hospital room, I could see how artful it was. I imagined these three teenagers grinning at one another in the Pelican Motel, mocking the vulnerable men they intended to fleece   I couldn't answer the one question I knew Andy would ask me: Why kill Mike? Why kill any of them? Thousands of men get swindled by scams like this every day of the year. It didn't have to come to murder.

I had a long drive home to think about it. I wouldn't be driving with my arm in a sling. Trujillo hooked me up with his younger cousin, who agreed to take me for a fee. Trujillo assures me Armando's a good kid. "Homey don't even carry a gat for protection," he told me.

Robb White

tomhaftmann.wixsite.com/robbtwhite

@tomhaftmann
@robbtwhite

Dead End

Every night he wakes me from my sleep and takes me to the cemetery. Intently focused, he drives his black hearse through the rust-twined gates, down the coiled dirt track, towards the earth's core. I can't get out, can't escape; there are no handles on the doors.

We bump past a mortuary located between the unmarked graves and baroque tombstones. He becomes distracted by a fluorescent stream of light coming from the window and pauses for a moment. Through the window we see a luminous Nicole Kidman in a lab coat, playing a starring role. She nonchalantly pulls rotting flesh from corpses and uses a bandsaw to extract marrow from the bones.

He refocuses and gains control. We move down the one-way track which deepens and narrows as it goes. He pulls up to an ashen-marble and coal mausoleum embossed with a crucifix and the moniker "Mortality" above the entryway, then makes me get out.

Burdened, with stooped shoulders and a cowered head, he pushes open the heavy door. He convoys me along a passage, points for me to sit and wait at the head of an embalmed cadaver. He carries in one hessian bag one after the other. Each was filled with dust, which he continually dumped at my feet. He labours and complains, but there is never enough decay to off-load. There is never enough he can do to show what is wrong with me.

After several hours of his contempt, just before daylight breaks, I feel that I can stand and make my way out. And as I do, I see the space reserved for me.

Sharon Willdin

www.sharonwilldin.com
@SharonWilldin
@sharonwilldinofficial

Polite

She could smell him. The odour was thick, cloying, an intruder in her nostrils. B.O., bacterial residue that had been squeezed from his skin and now sat rotting for all to bear. She turned her head towards him, a primal urge within her to ascertain the source of the foul odour. He was tall. Impossible so. With a mackintosh that reached his knees and no more. It hung open, a threadbare woollen vest over his protruding stomach. Three days' worth of bristle marred his face and, when he smiled at her, yellow and brown teeth – like piano keys – stared out at her from behind cracked lips.

She immediately turned toward the window and placed her bag on her knee, gripping it tightly. She watched him as he walked up the aisle, his reflection clear as the night was so dark outside and the lights inside the bus so bright. He chose a seat on the opposite end of the aisle, one row in front of her. She sighed. She could still smell him, but at least he wasn't sitting next to her.

She'd been to the sandwich bar down Maine Street to have a coke with the girls from her secretarial course. Although not one for a late evening – mother would worry and tomorrows laundry would still need ironed and folded away into her father's drawers – she was keen to make friends with the new girls she met. It had been a tough year for her. The flu that came to Antrack in South Carolina had been fierce, merciless and unholy. It took her sister, her best friend and the closest thing to an Aunt she'd ever had – Miss Harwell at the local elementary. These new girls in the city, a half hour down the road by bus, were to be a new start. And a night of cokes was a dream compared to the three funerals alone she'd attended in the past six months.

The bus jerked to a halt, throwing her violently forward and bringing her back to the present – though the smell of the strange man hadn't ever left her. An older woman with daisies in a basket and a small coin purse clutched in her gloved hand stood shakily from her seat and made her way towards the open door.

The cool night air was a God-send and she drank it down as best she could while shivering beneath her coat. She'd been silly, wearing it, but it was her best one, her very nicest coat and she'd wanted to make a good impression. By all accounts, it had worked. Two of the eight girls had remarked on how beautiful the ornate bumble buttons were and another one had ran her hand along her sleeve and cooed at how soft it was. It was barely October, she'd reasoned as her hopeful new friend ran her palm along her coat, and a little chill was barely a price to pay for new friends.

As the bus doors shut and the stench of the strange man once again occupied every particle of oxygen, she turned her head slightly and felt alone. Using her peripheral vision, she tried to take stock of the bus and realised that she was, in fact, alone but for the strange man and the bus driver. A gas station, its little shop lights dim with the late hour, pulled back from the bus and let the deep dark of the farmlands and countryside around them sink in. Her face was pale, she could see it clearly in the window. Her hair was limp, but still held in shape. Her lips were breaking, she noticed, under the constant assault she put them under from her own teeth. She looked at the man in the reflection and saw him staring back at her. His eyes met hers and he…though she couldn't be sure, not really…shook his head a little.

She threw her gaze to her lap and fiddled with her bag. Only after her breath had steadied did she once again look up at the window and search for if the man was still watching her.

He wasn't.

Instead, paper splayed out on his lap, he idly flicked through pages of black and white, the sound of rustling accompanying his awful smell like an old friend back from Vietnam. Pictures she couldn't quite make out blurred as he flicked his fingers through them. Only, and just for a moment, did his hand move other than to turn the page when his first finger traced what looked to be a mug shot of a man in the paper.

He turned to her again and, on seeing that she was staring at him, shook the paper closed and looked towards the bus driver as if he'd never been looking at the newspaper at all.

She tried to calm herself. Bad hygiene did not a pervert make, she tried to reason with herself. And even though he kept looking over at her, staring at her, she did wonder if perhaps it was her continual staring at him that was pricking an urgency within the strange man to turn towards her. Men and women alike always know when they are being watched. So, she tried not to look at him and reasoned that, should she glance around the bus, which was a perfectly reasonable thing to do as a single woman alone on a night bus, and he was looking at her then, well, then she would stand up and walk to the front of the bus and inform the driver.

Calming herself at her reasoning and the remembrance of the bus driver – meaning she was not alone – she looked for something to hold her attention for the twenty or so more minutes she'd have on the bus when it caught her eye.

At first, she presumed it was just the idle scratching's of a bored little boy on his mother's lap. But, as she looked more closely at it, she could see that someone had carved the shape of a star into the back of the seat in front of her. But, it wasn't a star, was it? No. She'd seen this particular star before and she knew it was no star at all. It was a pentagram. A symbol of the devil. But whoever had carved it had done so with unsteady hands as the lines connecting each of the five points were squint and hurried, several lines moving from one point to another in the hope that at least one of them would make it to its destination.

She felt the need to move seats bubble from the muscles in her thighs. But she didn't want to draw any attention to herself for fear that the strange man may take her movement as an indication that she wished to engage him in a conversation – a suggestion that would most certainly be false. She steading her breath by focusing on her mouth and the muscles that pulled the strange man's stinking air into her body and found she could taste blood. Whatever she'd been thinking upon seeing the pentagram had made her bite her lip and now a steady trickle of her own blood was pooling in her mouth beneath her tongue. She swallowed, careful not to make a gulping noise.

The strange man turned toward her. His face was hard now, no easy smile or angry look as she'd expect from a strange man on the night bus. He looked ready. For what she didn't know and it sent tingles down her neck and along her arms making her skin pull and the hairs on her arms raise. He shook his head again, this time leaving no doubt as to what he was doing. She couldn't turn from him. Not his gaze nor his person and so she stood.

Her legs shook but she stood all the same. This was silly now, ridiculous, she wouldn't be made to feel scared on her bus home. But she was. She moved past the man who now sat frozen, his eyes widened. Good, she thought. Now it's your turn to be afraid. She made past him and almost collapsed as his hand slithered along the bench he was sitting on – out of the driver's eye line – and tried to nip at her skirt. She jolted forward as the bus began to slow. To her surprise, she saw that her bus stop was just a few yards outside the bus windscreen and she could have wept with how relieved she was. But, before her hand could reach the driver's seat to warn him of the strange man, she felt him stand up behind her, his movement jostling the foul smell and making it fresh in her nose again as he released build ups from parts of his body that had been folded in on one another while he sat.

The bus door opened and she made to move down the steps and out into the night. The man behind her was committed to leaving the bus as she was and so she dithered.

"Evening, ma'am," the bus driver said. "Could you open this for me?"

He handed a flask over to her and she took it. The foul smelling strange man passed her, his hand on her lovely coat, his fingers tightening on the same sleeve her new friend had admired only a few hours before. But she pulled back and slipped free so the man stepped off the bus. She reasoned that he'd move on down the street and she could ask the driver to wait a moment so she could be sure he was gone before making the short trip home. But, as soon as the man was clear of the bus steps, the door closed shut and the bus began to move.

"Sit down, ma'am," the bus driver said as the foul-smelling man lunged at the closed doors. With his fists balled, he battered his weight against the bus doors, his eyes impossibly wide and his face turned ugly with hatred. Spittle flew from his mouth as the bus began to outpace him and as his face slipped from view she heard him shout, 'Get off.'

She was in such shock that she fell backwards onto the nearest seat and tried to martial her lips to utter a thank you to the bus driver who had just saved her life when it caught her eye. Just like before, a carving sat on the seat in front of the one she was sitting on. Another pentagram.

As she watched the bus pass her house, and the terror of the strange man fell on top of her, she wondered to herself, "who would have the time alone with a bus to engrave two pentagrams on it?"

Conner McAleese

@conner_mcaleese
@ConnerMcAleese

Dark Horse

The day I arrived at Riverside Academy there was a thunderstorm. The biggest one in the state in the last fifty years, according to the radio of my beat-up old Kia Rio. It lasted for almost a full day and into the night - tornado watches and all of that - the blackness only enhancing the sharp glow of the electricity coursing through the air.

I had never seen anything like it, and it was magnificent.

Pulling my car over to the side of the highway, I stood on the edge of town, rain pelting against my back and soaking through the fabric of my faded burgundy hoodie, my ponytail not doing a whole hell of a lot at keeping my hair out of my face. I shielded my camera as best as I could, long strands whipping against my cheeks and getting stuck in the strap, but I knew I had gotten the perfect angle for the perfect shot - and then it hit in the field right in front of my face.

Boom.

Click.

The sky loomed grey and heavy above me as I tucked the camera under my shirt and tripped my way back to the driver's side door of the Kia. A gust of wind almost caught me, but I slammed the door shut on it and exhaled, the vehicle rocking around me like a great, metal dome.

A car beeped at me as it drove by, road water splashing against my windshield, blurring my vision of the drive ahead. I flicked my wipers on, simultaneously with my blinker, and eased my way back out onto the road, empty except for that one person ahead of me up over the hill.

I had never felt so wild and so free.

The weather is always an interesting thing to photograph, in my opinion. It's one of the most frequently photographed things in existence, seeing as it exists in every outdoor picture. However, I like to focus specifically on events - hurricanes, rain, interesting clouds - to draw focus to the way we hardly notice that the world changes so frequently around us.

Those pictures, in conjunction with that concept, got me here, to Riverside Academy.

My phone beeps in my pocket as I walk out of class, a day just like any other, the sunlight shining through the side window of Riverside and piercing my corneas with lemony brightness. I wrangle the device from my back pocket, nearly dropping my bag on the floor, while swiping the screen open and reading the text it contains.

'you done with my copy of that awful book everyone hates?'

I smirk at my screen.

Dillon Crewe and I instantly bonded upon my arrival at Riverside, both socially awkward photographers with no set friend group and no particular direction. I'm honestly a little jealous of Dillon's understated elegance in his photography - his macro work is something to be admired even though he doesn't seem to find anything special about it.

Art - the hardest profession in the world, according to Rent the Musical.

'in my room - want me to go get it? Meet you in the parking lot in five'

'roger that'

The book he's talking about that everyone hates is actually one of my favourites, Wuthering Heights by Emily Bronte. I seem to have misplaced my copy back home in Vermont and when Dillon received a copy to read as an assignment for his English class I couldn't help but bribe him to let me read it as well. I love getting lost in the story of Catherine and Heathcliff - there's something romantic and timeless about their relationship in its ultimate sadness.

The dormitories are matching brick buildings to the right side of the main campus - or left, depending on what direction you're facing. They both have matching decorative gates, the same front patch of hostas growing out of control along the walkways, and twin monumental plates affixed and ascribed to the edifices denoting that the school is sponsored by the Riverside family. The only difference between the two is that a poster about Kelsey O'Flaherty is still pasted in the glass of the girls' dorms, her black hair and dark eyes jumping out of the page despite its age and wear.

Kelsey would have known the answer to his question in class today. She probably would have been paying attention the whole time instead of being distracted, as I'm being now.

Unfortunately, every time I walk into this building, I can't help but notice the poster.

There are a few of them left, still posted around town and on campus like casual observers of the life she left behind. We had been best friends, meeting on my first day at Riverside and forming an inseparable friendship until her disappearance. It's hard not to feel like she's still around - her face on blaring white stock paper. Kelsey was a photographer as well, a talented one with an eye for portraits, something some of our professors, Mr. Leighton more exactly, may have mentioned a time or two in class in passing. He always speaks of her with such a melancholy tone I know that either something happened between the two of them or she was really just that gifted in the art of photo taking. That's one thing Kelsey never told me about.

She went missing a year ago now and no sign of her has been found. Speculation has dwindled to her taking off for New York, away from her abusive father under a new name nobody would recognize. The police here have all but stopped looking for her, nobody pushing the search forward with their demands for a missing daughter. I never wanted to give up on Kelsey, but maybe I didn't know her as well as I thought I did.

'you coming? you said five min...'

Dillon isn't exactly patient.

'yes just getting your book hold your horses'

'i dont have any horses you know that ethan'

Dillon's book is face-down on my bed where I left it, my wall of weather photographs taking over the space to the far side of my bed. I can recall every moment that each of those snapshots was taken - but my favourite is still the lightning picture I got on the side of the road my first day here. There's something ominous about the texture of the electricity against the black sky, it almost looks as if the entire thing is devoid of colour - which it isn't.

I grab the paperback off the disheveled fleece sheets and stuff it into my bag with my camera.

'coming'

Dillon responds almost immediately.

'bring your camera - something cool is happening'

The first time I see the black horse outside of a dream, I don't think anyone else notices she's there. But as I bring Dillon's copy of Wuthering Heights to him I watch her trot to the edge of the parking lot and toss her mane, the ebony strands flashing the sunlight and sucking up the brightness into an overcast grey. I actually look twice because in the first instance I, myself, don't believe that horse is running around outside of Riverside Academy; the nearest farm is far out into the junction of two townships at least a half an hour from here.

"Do you see them? Did you bring your camera?" Dillon calls to me across the parking lot and I'm certain his voice is going to spook the mare. However, before I can hush him I find that my concern is unnecessary - she continues munching away on the tendrils of grass behind Dillon's black Santa Fe as if nothing has happened in the world around her. On my approach she raises her head, blinks at me, and walks off silently through the trees.

Dillon doesn't see the horse.

He's pointing at the sky where mammatus clouds are hanging, orb-like, with a smoky black colouring indicative of upcoming weather. The pouches are tinged in a soggy yellow, a thick haze crackling through the air, and for the first moment since I've stepped outside I notice the rapid change in the temperature.

It feels hot. But not summertime hot, rather like I'm standing in the middle of my mother's beef stew and the vegetables are simmering around my body.

"Wanna go take some photos?" Dillon breaks up my occupation and sends it to dissipate, wrestling the book from between my fingers and tossing it on the back seat of his SUV through an open window. He has a playful smile and a cautious demeanour that sometimes make me forget about everything that's gone wrong in my day. And between them both and with his passion for art, Dillon eats away at my heart in a way only a boy from California can.

I stare at the spot where the horse used to be, the empty greenery rustling around the silhouette of Dillon's blonde hair. I strain my eyes to look in between the branches and stretch my hearing as best I can along the symphony of Riverside sounds in aims of confirming my horse-related delusion.

"Ethan?"

"Did you see that horse?" The words tumble out of my mouth before I have a chance to stop them.

Dillon wrinkles his forehead.

"What?"

I realize in that second how insane I sound, trying to gobble the words back up out of their exposure.

"Nothing, I said of course - you know, to the taking photos idea." Small beads of perspiration dot the back of my neck and I try to swipe them away as nonchalantly as I can.

Get a grip, Ethan.

Dillon flashes me his signature grin - the one that probably made Lilah develop her crush on him in the first place.

"Well, hop in. I'll take you to the edge of the mountains and maybe we can get some cool contrast."

He flings open his door and clambers into the front seat, turning the engine over before I have a chance to move my feet.

"Time's ticking, E. I can only hold those horses for so long."

"What?"

I open the passenger's side door and take up my usual seat, slipping my digital camera onto the floor mat.

"Earlier. You texted me and said to hold my horses. I've held them all I can. Let's get out of here."

A tiny wave of relief washes over me as we pull out of the parking lot, and Dillon flicks on the radio to drown our silence. I recognize the song but I couldn't tell you the name, even once I start tapping my fingers along the windowsill with the drum beat.

Another thing I love about Dillon - he doesn't feel the need to fill every silence. We can comfortably just be. It's an assuring and terrifying thing all wrapped up in one commodity.

We drive fifteen minutes north, out of Riverside and up into Eisan where the mountains start to appear in the background. They form broad points against the monochrome of the outside, edged shapes in the landscape poking up into the pouches protruding from the atmosphere. It's an interesting texture, and so I snap a couple of shots of Dillon driving, the clouds and thunderheads bristling in the distance, the glass of the windshield reflecting the tiny bit of leftover light. Not quite Faces Magazine quality, but portfolio-worthy nonetheless.

Dillon must be able to read my goddamn mind.

"I hear you haven't handed in your Faces submission yet."

"Hell, who told you that?" I slap my hand against my thigh and drop the camera into my lap.

"Giselle. Asked for my help and I told her you were better to ask. She mentioned you weren't done either."

"Ugh. Got the lecture already from Mr. Leighton." I roll my eyes.

"Elliott's a good guy, E. He sees something in your work." There's a precarious pause. "So do I."

A pinkish hue creeps from my chest up my pale skin to my cheeks.

"Thanks." I feel so stupid not knowing what else to say. Dillon doesn't respond any further, interrupted by a light but hammering rain beginning to pound on the windshield. A half a mile up the road is a pit stop with a couple of picnic tables and we travel amidst the lyrics of a song I definitely don't know.

The tires of the Santa Fe crunch in the gravel as Dillon pulls off the road and turns off the car. A deep, throaty rumble hits us, thundering sky-hooves of a thousand black horses. The mammatus clouds look heavier here, somehow, the deep rippled groove between each pursing like a dark and endless river.

"Just in time for the show." Ethan reclines his seat slightly while I crawl halfway out the passenger's side window to sit on the ledge. Rain slides down my arms, soaking through my shirt and dripping down the ends of my hair as I rest my elbows on the roof of the SUV, camera steady on the surface.

Boom.

Click.

Dillon drives us back to Riverside amidst a downpour to drown the entire town.

As luck would have it, the sky opens up after I've snapped my first ten photos and I'm forced to give up my position on the side of the vehicle to something less likely to attract both electricity and illness. I roll up the window to the Santa Fe, feeling a bit defeated, flicking through the shots I've managed to capture on my old Canon digital camera. Dillon blasts the heat in a desperate attempt to dry me out while my hair speckles the interior with water.

"Get anything good?"

We're almost back at the school before he speaks, the road noise, patter of rain, and crumbling thunder orchestrating a melody to soothe us in our return.

The wipers make a slapping noise.

"Hard to tell until I get them on the big screen. Everything looks alright on a small display."

Dillon smirks.

Slap, slap, slap.

"So what's with the hard time on the Faces project? I would have figured you'd have tons of inspiration."

"Dillon, I photograph the weather, not people. I don't particularly like most of them. They're so - ... I don't know. People-y."

He laughs and I laugh with him.

"I don't know, E. You're creative. I thought you'd have so many ideas based on this year's theme."

Slap, slap, slap.

"*Tessellations*? That's not a theme, that's someone playing with their online thesaurus."

Dillon punches me in the arm with one hand and uses the other to turn the SUV into the Riverside parking lot. He turns off the engine and the wipers cease their noise. The outside, however, does not; the rain falling in king-sized sheets along the pavement.

"Well, what's your submission then, genius?"

Dillon straightens up in his seat, unbuckling himself.

"I did macro work of networking patterns in plant life."

"What the shit, Dillon? That's brilliant." I can't help the groan that escapes my lips. "How the hell am I going to beat that?"

"It's all about perspective and how you spin the story. Remember the explanation is forty percent of the actual judging mark."

I forgot that part but I have no intention of mentioning it out loud. A photograph is one thing but an insightful explanation is another - I'm neither a strong nor an interesting writer. And, on top of that, I don't even have an idea to write about.

Dillon and I sit amidst the tranquility of the car and the rhythm of the noise outside, watching the water gather in lumpy ripples on the windows before falling off to meet the ground.

I can feel my heart beating in my chest.

Lub dub. Lub dub. Lub dub.

This silence is different. I don't know the words for it but I'm sure I could photograph it and you'd see it in our expressions. Our past couple of outings have ended in this way - a quiet moment in one of our vehicles with neither of us having any idea of what to do next. It's an indecision that haunts me now, every time I see Dillon, that eventually we're going to have to say goodbye and it doesn't seem either of us wants to.

We both speak at the same time, cutting off our sentences at equally timed intervals.

"I should go-..."

"Ethan, I think that-..."

Dillon gives me that crooked smile again and if I wasn't already such a mess with pre-occupation, I probably would have turned into a puddle right there on the floor mat.

"You go first," he offers.

"It doesn't look like the rain's going to let up. Should we make a run for it?"

Dillon looks outside with a twisted glance, then turns back to me, his bottom lip red from the pressure of his teeth clenching into it.

"Yeah." He unlocks the doors to the SUV. "On three?"

I tuck my camera underneath my already soaked shirt, offering it what little protection I can provide.

"One, two -..."

"Three!" I yell the word and sprint from the car, crashing through the raindrops. I hear Dillon lock the automatic doors with a distant beep, my footsteps and thumping heart the only soundtrack to my journey back to the sleeping quarters across the quad. Rain rips past me, splattering along my face, Dillon nipping at my heels, but my head start is just a little too much for him to overtake.

We gather at the door for the girls' quarters, Kelsey's eyes piercing us from her watchful poster. I breathe hard from the exercise only to have the air catch in my throat when I look up at Dillon and spot his shirt sticking to him in all the right places.

He knows I'm looking.

Kelsey's hair in the poster behind him looks like the mane of the black horse I saw earlier in the parking lot. And the eyes - they're like two deep constellations in Atlantis, scraping away at the tessellated bits of my soul.

And then inspiration smashes into me, a lightning strike on my brain.

"Did you see a horse earlier?" I snap my eyes back to meet Dillon's and his face crumples.

"What? When we were out at the stop?"

"No, in the parking lot. I saw a horse. A mare. She was black; thick mane -..." I cut myself off once I notice Dillon's confusion, the expression marked all over him.

He responds slowly, carefully, as if he is evaluating my sanity.

"You saw a horse in the parking lot?"

I nod.

"Ethan, are you on something?"

I shake my head, droplets of leftover rain splattering, dotting the dry concrete of the overhang. A grin crawls its way over my face and I adjust the camera still under my shirt, looking at Dillon then back at the photo of Kelsey.

"Listen, I think I have an idea. For the Faces Magazine project. I'll talk to you later, alright?"

Before Dillon has a chance to respond I've taken off into the rain, thunder rolling from somewhere back in Eisan, shaking up the synapses of my imagination.

I'm still awake at two in the morning, posters of Kelsey littering my floor, a veritable carpet of sleepless artistry. Out in the hallway I can hear a group of girls just getting in from some party they drove up to in Broughton, their slurred voices and cliche laughter stirring in my ears. I'm half out of bed because I need the extra time to put together my idea, and the other half because I'm so exhausted from having a repetitive dream about the cottage in the woods that I can't bear to be stuck in it again.

"Elliott is so into you, Lacey - I swear."

Giggling ensues, hushed by one of the members of the gaggle whose voice I can't interpret from behind the blockade of my door. Keys jingle and doors open and shut. I can't picture Mr. Leighton wanting anything to do with those three. An adult man definitely has more sense than that. Especially one that was a part of the military.

I hope.

Oh dear God, I truly hope.

I shake my head from side to side, trying to expel the thought from in between my ears. A few seconds pass before I regain equilibrium abs dig into my pile of photos, pen poised in my hand and a notebook atop one of my only empty carpet squares. The proper words to describe what I'm doing absolutely elude me, and I'm forced into a hypertensive brainstorm, scribbling with everything I've got.

The idea starts in the middle, with Kelsey's disappearance, and branches out into reverberations of the impact. I can make a spider's web of the correlation of events - from the way I felt the moment I saw her empty room to the vigil at Riverside that was held in an attempt to build the school back up and jigsaw together all the pieces of Kelsey's life without her. Some concepts are corner pieces, some edges, some confused and connected in the middle with nowhere to start on their position but a sea of the same colour in various shades.

I need to start with the corner pieces. I need something tangible to work with and I look up at the ceiling for divine intervention. My fairy lights twinkle in the haphazard darkness, exuding pale yellow pinpricks of light along the walls next to my bed. Reflections of the bulbs play off the glossy finish of my walk of photographs, interrupting the snapshot with unintended abrasions.

Hauling myself from the mess to sit on my patchwork quilt, I survey the room and listen to the sounds of the campus in the night. The hum of the girls still exists from Lacey's room across the hall, but the other side of my room is quiet - the dorm on my left empty of a body but filled with possessions of Kelsey's that nobody's ever thought about getting rid of and her family has never come to pick up. It only further supports the idea that Kelsey's father was an abusive son of a bitch who didn't give a shit about the only O'Flaherty daughter.
And then, another thought tickles me.

My first corner piece, my first connection with the tessellation of Kelsey, is in her room.

She gave me the extra key to her dorm about three months before she went missing, and I dig under some books on my nightstand to locate it. The metal is warm against my fingers, and I dig the ridges into my palm as I stand, listening at my door for anyone out meandering in the halls.

Silence.

My door opens with a tiny wail, imperceptible even in the quiet, the central air system running a soft hum in the background and serving as a kind of white noise machine for the dormitory floor. I creep out into the hall and finger Kelsey's key into the lock, the metal scraping inside the knob before twisting open.

Muggy air hits me in the face and the smell of Kelsey's vanilla perfume permeates the air. Somehow after all this time it still hasn't dissipated.

I close the door behind me, leaning against the coolness of the surface, and breathe in the familiar scent and absorb the weight of being in her room again. I'd come here once before, right after she went missing and the police tape was all over the place, the yellow warning of the ribbon doing nothing to deter me from taking a look over the space that had belonged to my friend.

Honestly, I'm a little surprised that the room hasn't been cleaned out, disinfected, and assigned to a new student. I can only imagine that this hasn't been the case due to the open file with the police department, although nothing's moved forward on it in months.

The moonlight from the window shines a beacon on Kelsey's desk, the curtains drawn away from the glass and allowing the night to saturate her belongings in a creamy peace. I pad across the beige shag rug in the middle of Kelsey's room, the furry fingers of the fabric squashing beneath my feet and cushioning my heels. Her computer sits, blank, next to a pile of photographs, a bracelet, a cup of fine-point markers, and a chess piece.

I stop, dead.

A black horse.

I can't believe what I'm seeing and because of it I shake my head from side to side again, trying to clear the clouds from my mind. But when I'm done twisting and nodding to and fro the knight's piece is still there, etched in black glass, bouncing the early morning essence off its surface. A lovely coincidence, I tell myself, just a tiny piece of an interesting memory.

There is a desperate need to touch the horse. I lift it off the desk, heavier than I expected, a little ring shaped like a zero left in the settled dust next to Kelsey's laptop. It rolls over in my hand, the ears of the statuette poking at my palm.

I think I'll keep her.

I lock Kelsey's room back up, closing the darkness and the stars within her walls, leaving her bracelet and her photos and the vanilla smell behind me for another night, another time, some point when I need more closure. I place the glass horse on my windowsill and she sparkles an ebony elixir, the moon broad on her back like a rotund saddle.

There's something beautiful about the serenity of it all.

I pick up my camera, framing the horse and the sill in a bath of light, off-siding the framework to pixelate everything beyond the window.

Something is missing. The capture is too empty, to plain and black and dismal. And although this feeling is easily reciprocated on film and on a digital photograph, I want something less cliche - something that doesn't scream teenager and instead screams, well, tessellation. The interconnected network of it all.

Placing the camera back on the bookshelf, I lower myself onto the floor into the middle of my fire hazard. Barely a moment passes by when my phone buzzes, a tiny tone coordinating with the mechanical movement and scaring the hell out of me. I grab it from atop my bed, as if the noise is going to wake up my nonexistent neighbour.

It's Dillon.

'you awake?'

I glance at the time on the top of my screen. 2:33am and counting.

'mhmmmm'

'good - im coming over'

'Dillon I'm working'

'nothing good happens after midnight E - see you in a min'

So much for nothing good happening after midnight.

I flop down on the bed underneath the fairy lights, my hair getting tangled in with my multitude of pillows and blankets. The picture I took my first day at Riverside is next to my face as I turn to the wall, flanked by a photo of me with Kelsey, another I took of Dillon when he was fiddling with his own camera, and a selfie I took on a day I bothered to do my makeup. Some days it's hard to get motivated.

Most days I feel like I'm walking around in a fog - like my mind belongs somewhere else and my body is just a placeholder for something better.

The constant changes in the Riverside weather at least make me feel alive.

I don't know how long I lie there, underneath the tiny lights, before a soft knock raps at my door. It's unlocked so I simply stretch my arm out and open the latch, a triangle of incandescent light seeping onto the floor and blaring into my eyes. Dillon takes a half a step in and steps on a crumpled mass of Kelsey-covered papers.

"What the hell happened in here?"

I leap off the bed to usher him in, shushing his voice with an annoying sound of my own.

"People are sleeping, you know."

Dillon raises an eyebrow, kicking his shoes off in the entry.

"You mean like Lacey and her minions? They're drunk as hell."
There's a twinge in his voice that tells me something I can't decide if I
want to know.

"And how do you know this?" I return to my seat on the bed and
Dillon crawls up next to me, parking himself in the corner and resting his
shoulders against the juncture in the walls.

"I was there."

I roll my eyes and sigh.

"You're here because you're drunk."

"I'm here because I'm worried about you. You kind of went off
earlier."

I shuffle the papers along the carpet with my feet, making a
space for me to stand.

"I'm fine, really. Just - all this is getting to me, you know.
Kelsey, you, the competition - ..."

"Hold up. What did I do?" Dillon sits up straight and adjusts his
position on the bed.

*Oh shit, did I say out loud that he's getting to me? Good luck
playing this one off, Ethan.*

"Nothing, nothing about you. That's not what I meant." I can
feel my insides collapsing in on themselves as I try to formulate a lie.

"E, I'm drunk. But I'm not that drunk."

My hands make their way to my hips, unimpressed.

"Dillon, you texted me at almost three in the morning. You're
that drunk."

He bites his bottom lip and heaves a heavy, growling breath.

"Fine, I'm drunk. But you're not working and I'm not leaving."

I sigh, knowing he's got me, and plunk myself back down on the bed. I don't know how one person can manage to make so much since when they've been drinking, but Dillon seems capable of carrying it all. I think about the Ziploc bag of marijuana in my nightstand and contemplate the ramifications of rolling some out. There aren't any.

"Wanna get high?"

I reach over the bed, scooting myself up to the nightstand, pulling open the drawer. A Saturday morning at 3am - after a week of hell and a day of having delusions about horses - seems like the perfect time to get ripped and think up a drug-induced project with the theme tessellation. Dillon raises his eyebrow, pausing at my question for only a second.

"Fine. But I'm rolling. You're shit at it."

He takes the papers out of my hand, picking up a copy of Peter Pan from somewhere beneath my covers, and starts to crush up his selection of buds from the bag.

Dillon's right, I'm bad at rolling. He has more dexterous fingers than I do.

I watch him with a manic fascination, as if I'm looking at a miracle being performed right in front of my own eyes. He knows I'm observing it all, a rabid curiosity and carnal desire to get the drug in my system. He also knows how I get when I'm high - most of the reason he probably agreed to smoke in the first place.

I slide off the bed, Dillon's warmth near behind me, and slip open the window above my futon. I've reaped the benefits of having a corner room - an extra window - and he sits facing me, a lighter already ablaze. We rest there in silence, passing the joint back and forth, waiting expectantly for the minute I start to fall apart.

Dillon picks up the glass horse.

I am greedy with my hits on the joint and so Dillon rolls another few in the time it takes me to finish the first. The cover of Peter Pan is dusty with green and the bottom of the horse has served as a tamper for the outer shells of the buds.

She doesn't seem to mind.

The glass glitters the tiny red nip of the end of the joint, my bedroom concocting a veritable mixture of oxygen, smoke, and dramatic allure. I pull a fleece throw over my bare legs, the jean shorts I was wearing earlier doing nothing for warmth and flick the end of the stick out the window. The ash floats away into the darkness and I snub the end, dropping the filter down into the grass.

Dillon hands me another, and I just hold it for a minute.

"You know, I think I might just have something for Faces."

The words are punctuated with a cough and the joint is removed from my fingers and nestled between Dillon's. The world moves at a leisurely pace, the air outside seeping a melting indigo that paints the inside of my dorm. Peter Pan is on the floor. The horse is back on the windowsill.

"And what's that, then?"

Dillon's voice is raspy as he reclines against the arm of the futon, the lit stick pursed between his lips as he stretches out his shoulders.

He takes up more space than I remember.

"Kelsey's disappearance."

Dillon gives an awkward look, passing the joint over to me again.

"How's that a tessellation?"

He blows a smoke ring toward the general direction of the window.

"How isn't it? She's left little fragments of herself behind."

"You're taking the most macabre angle possible, aren't you?"

I take a hit, sucking the smoke deep down into my bronchioles and feeling it burn. My eyes are hazy with pinpricks of coal coloured light as I pass the rest back to Dillon, who has already started on another. He puts both in his mouth and hits them, hard, breathing in a long and drawn out inhale that goes on and on and on. One joint goes out; finished.

I start to laugh, the high taking me over. My body feels so much more relaxed than it did at the end of the day in Leighton's class - my anxiousness about Lacey and her minions and Faces and Kelsey seeping into my ruby red painted toes.

"It's about the network."

"What network?"

I sigh, muddling the words.

"You know, like we learned from that anthropologist about the tribe who believes you leave an invisible connection between yourself and everyone you meet."

Dillon closes his eyes for so long I think he's passed out.

"Dillon?"

"Shh, E. I'm thinking."

A minute goes by. Then five. Then I look at the clock and it's 3:41am.

"Still thinking?"

The words separate themselves from my body and I can see them floating in the air, multicoloured, where they hang before popping like soap bubbles.

Pop. Pop.

Dillon shudders, taking a long drag and finishing off the joint himself. The rolled drug is barely lit any more and so I don't know what Dillon is breathing in other than remnants of a potential high.

"Thinking about how beautiful you are."

Here we go.

I try and visit this version of Dillon every once and awhile, a morbid need for his intoxicated body and a fascination with the feeling of him when I finally relax. The drugs free us - providing a barrier for an actual conversation about emotions - but allowing some momentary pleasure in our own indecision.

My skin responds quickly to the feeling of Dillon crawling over to me and it's like a cool rush blows over me, the earliest of the morning birds whistling and singing in the Riverside darkness. There is an unlimited stillness in my room, a smoky residue drifting along the windowsill side of the space, the black horse watching over our bodies as they meld together at the moment Dillon's lips crash themselves with the gentleness of a virgin, into my own.

He tastes like how I remember he tastes, despite the fact that I can't remember the last time that we both got high and had each other. It couldn't have been long ago, because of the familiarity, but it has been enough time amid sessions that I feel itchy and anxious.

My back sinks into the cushions of the futon as Dillon roams. I pull his shirt up over his head with a severe lack of dexterity, but his eyes are so red in the moonlight that I don't think he notices my fumbling. My stomach growls in the nightfall and he smiles into my mouth, slipping his tongue against mine as my fingers grapple with the hem of his jeans.

Dillon's gentleness fades into a pernicious desire, fingers wrapping into hair and pulling my head back for his lips to prowl along the sensitive parts of my throat. A heavy heat suckles along my toes and inches up my legs, resting in between my thighs.

Then, there is fire and water and waves, and I am lost.

We stumble on each other in the thick of the radiance of the early day, a tangle of arms and high and emotions and inhibition. I see fields of lupins, and rabbits, and a house on the side of the beach and Dillon gnarls into my ear. I bring my arm up to pull him into me and I knock the black horse off its lounge on the window, sending it tumbling into the darkness of the outside.

The effects of the marijuana halt - immediate.

"Hang on," I whisper, shuffling my way from underneath Dillon. He has a sheen of perspiration and his denims are crumpled down by his ankles, thigh muscles furrowing with impatience.

"E?" His voice is deeper than usual.

"The horse fell out the window."

Dillon's face falls - a moment of realization. He is reminded of my visions, I can tell just by the way his eyes change as they leak their concern into my own.

"The horse?" He chokes the words out, voice cracking, but letting me out from the prison of his arms.

"Yeah, Kelsey's horse. I knocked it out the window. I have to go get it."

Throughout the duration of my so-called life, I've become extraordinarily adept at ruining the moment.

Dillon rolls back onto the opposite side of the futon as I madly scramble out the door, silent on the outside but crashing and impatient on the inside. My bare feet pad against the hallway carpet as I take the stairs one flight down to ground level, pushing open the heavy door. I am encased in the crickets, toads, and ephemeral evening, clad only in a pair of black boy-short underwear and a navy blue tank top. My bra straps slip over my shoulders with every movement of my arms; loosened.

I stare up at the side of the brick dorm. My windows are the only ones lit up this time of night - or morning, depending on your perspective - a glaring yellow shadowed by Dillon. He watches me in concentrated frustration, an ice cube in a desert storm, and I can feel his eyes piercing holes in the backdrop of the rising sun.

I don't care.

The gardens surrounding the sleeping quarters are vast, tinged in lavender and rose, algae green and robin's egg blue, to form an ocean of wild colours. Directly underneath my room is a patch of lambadas, careful flowers with cotton candy petals. One is squished and broken with the weight and impact of the glass horse.

She calls to me.

Over here, Ethan. Here I am.

I traipse through the dirt, squelching the peat moss and mulch between my toes. Trying not to step on any of the flowers, I pluck the chess piece from the gardens. She's wet with morning dew and I dry her on my shirt.

It's only ten steps back to the doorway but to my left the branches of the old coniferous trees rustle. I snap my eyes over to the general direction, peering into the darkness, able to immediately ascertain I'm still alone. I half expect to see the black horse tossing her mane in between the trunks. Instead I pull the door back open, my wet feet silently caressing the carpet.

Dillon meets me in the hall. He's fully dressed, his hair mussed in choppy pieces, a pair of shoes shamefully in his left hand.

"I'm gonna go back to my room." He barely looks at me. I wish I had the ability to know what was going on in his head but when I try to project myself into his body I keep coming up blank.

"No, no - please don't leave." The words sound stupider as I spell them between us, and instead of popping into nothingness they twist and twirl in a hazy smoke that lingers. Fingers swipe through it, dissipating the assorted alphabet into the night.

My voice must be louder than it sounds because Dillon motions for me to keep it down. I grab his hand and pull him back into my room, crumpling the Kelsey papers as I shut and lock the door.

"Ethan, come on." Dillon's feet are planted firmly at the entryway.

"I just had to go -..."

"Please. Don't." He raises one palm to me. "Something weird is going on with you, E."

The honesty is appreciated but I can't find a way to acknowledge the truth in his accusation. Something abnormal tickles at the depths of my mind and my hand holding the chess piece tingles, a mild heat crawling its way along my palm. My hand pulses and I switch the horse from one to the other.

"Just - ugh. I'm sorry. Stay. We'll smoke the rest of the weed and watch the sun come up. It's Saturday. We can watch movies." I am grasping at poorly placed, but all too familiar, straws.

It's impossible to tell if Dillon likes or abhors this idea. I don't get the chance to visually interpret the effect of my comments. The world has turned into a series of squiggly lines and a dull ache in my appendages that throbs with each beat of my heart. I drop the horse on the bed and slide my way across the sheets on my hands and knees before crumpling into a tired ball of delusion.

I hear a sigh, soft, amidst the walls. The light turns off and Dillon drops his shoes, a crinkling noise from where they hit papers littered with information on Kelsey. She makes a snowy, white carpet on top of my rug and Dillon doesn't bother kicking the pages out from underneath his toes. He folds himself into my bed and rests his chin on my head.

"I wish I understood what's been going on with you today, E." I can feel his gentled honesty wrapping tendrils around my body, holding me captive. There is an itching sensation of wanting a blanket, only for a second, because Dillon reads my mind and pulls a fleece throw over our bottom halves. I snuggle into the fabric, and therefore, into him in an acutely confusing display of affection.

"I'm fine."

I say it full well knowing that the phrase is one that is said both in candor and subtle, hinting fallacy.

Dillon pulls the horse from a rimple of the blankets, reaching over me to set her on the nightstand. A smudged drop of dew still rests between the rise of her ears, missed by his fingers and my shirttail.

She stares at me, but I can't do anything about it.

"You're not fine, Ethan."

There's something about the conversation that declines to hold me hostage. I feel Dillon roll onto his back to stare up at the ceiling, the fairy lights, and the reflection of the bulbs on the glossy surface of the photo wall.

I fall asleep, tumbling into a deep, indigo thickness.

What feels like instantly, I'm walking up a forest path in the midst of a hurricane, wind whipping around my arms, scratching at the spots my forlorn jacket would normally bandage. The infinitesimal rain barges against the soaking fabric of my clothes, pounding into my jeans, my socks, my shoes, squelching in the grass and the mud and under my toes.

Up ahead is a cottage in the woods.

Dillon isn't there when I wake up from my cottage dream. Glancing at the time on my phone I realize it's only a few hours after we both passed out - lethargic in our mutual high alongside the rising lemonade sky and flossy clouds. The morning is vast and unyielding, as all mornings are, opening the world up to another collection of possibilities in any one of an innumerable amount of random intervals. Birds play along the field lines, drifting up toward Eisan, and the storminess of the day before is washing away and blowing out to the ocean. It looks like the beginning of yesterday, before all the mammatus clouds rolled in.

The spot next to me in the bed hasn't retained any of Dillon's warmth. It's as if he was never there at all. Judging by the tiny path carved in Kelsey's posters, it is safe for me to assume that he departed not long after I drifted off, taking care not to wake me.

There's something sweet about that gesture. Something I wish we had the backbone to talk to each other about when we aren't in a state of total inebriation.

I drag myself out of bed to the sound of birds and switch off the fairy lights overhead. I'm still wearing my clothes from yesterday but I can't be bothered to change them when I'm only going to sit on my floor and think, so I make the executive decision not to bother - at least not yet anyway. I have too much work to do if I want to get my Faces Magazine submission in on time, and also if I want to be able to get Mr. Leighton off my case before class on Monday.

My room smells like a combination of marijuana, stale beer, and vanilla. Once I place all the scents I am smashed in the face with the reality of last night, and the recollection that I need something more of Kelsey's to add to the tessellation-network-photo collage that is sitting in my brain.

Out of habit rather than necessity, I listen at my door before I open it, hoping to avoid Lacey and her minions if any of them happen to be out and about.

There is thankful silence.

The hallway is deserted when I look down toward the washroom corridors. A quiet turning of a handle slips into my ear, and Kelsey's door opens.

"Ethan," Jason nods toward me, a sheepish look painted on his face.

"What are you doing in Kelsey's room?"

If he notices I'm wearing the same clothes from yesterday he doesn't acknowledge it.

"It's hard to explain." The words come stammering out of Jason's mouth as searches for just the right ones.

I stare. That's the only description I have for the face that I'm making - a poignant stare that waits for a better answer.

"It's like this." He shoves his hands into his pockets. "Before Lacey and I were together, Kelsey and I were ... *a thing*."

I bite the inside of my cheek.

"It's stupid, okay? Lacey would kill me if she knew I wasn't totally over this whole Kelsey disappearance thing. But we used to sit on the roof and watch the cars pass by and just talk about life, you know. The interconnectedness of it all."

"I get that. My Faces Magazine submission is kind of along the same lines. A loose translation of tessellation. And Kelsey, I suppose."

Jason smiles.

"Clever girl. I might be able to help you with that - I've got soccer but come by my place later. I've got a few things of hers you might be able to use as inspiration."

"Thanks."

We are sucked into another silent period.

"Listen, I know you guys were best friends. If you know anything..."

"I don't know anything, Jason."

I switch uncomfortably from foot to foot.

"Okay. Well, thanks. Don't tell the cops I was in there." Jason bobs his head back in the direction of the door and I scoff. We both grin - the police are never coming back here looking for Kelsey.

"Good enough."

Jason saunters off, down the hall and through the doors to the stairs. I think about going back into Kelsey's room but then I remember what Jason said about the roof. Maybe the top of the girls' dorm could have something to do with my Faces submission - just another piece of Kelsey that is taped together over this entire town.

The door upstairs is in the middle of the hallway along the far wall, indicated in a clashing mauvey-rose facade. Usually the entryway and that section of stairwell are kept locked, but to my own benefit the last person up there didn't bother to close up. I can't help but wonder if it was Kelsey and Jason, even though the timeline doesn't fit.

The door to the roof opens with a whine, interjecting dissatisfaction on my plan to stand out in the world. Beams of light shine brightly on my skin, and I prop the door open with a discarded brick to allow myself back inside.

The tips of my fingers and my toes start to tingle. I'm not scared of being up so high, per se, but the flatness of the roof combined with the starkness of the distant fields creates a mind game of a flat plain that continues on. I could almost swear it did continue forever - like I could step off the roof and onto the next.

Cars crawl past in a typical Saturday fashion, a little busier than most weekends. Riverside isn't exactly a bustling metropolis - but Kia Rios and Honda Civics and other vehicles I can't possibly name make their way through campus. Destination unknown.

I peer shakily down at the campus, light refracting off glossy surfaces, and think about Kelsey. She must have done some beautiful artwork up here, away from the noise of the rest of the world. There's no helping my head as I picture her and Jason, sitting along the edge of the roof, legs dangling over the corners. And despite my numb appendages, I sit there too.

Time passes, as it does.

Then I see the horse. She's in the middle of the road.

The black of the horse's hide glistens with the early sunlight, a midnight canvas against a backdrop of emerald, sand, and bits of mahogany tree bark. She tosses her mane in an elegant and refined fashion as she trots down the yellow double line. Traffic has dissipated around the mare, weaving appropriately to avoid her existence, and she appears unaffected by the noise of the road or the movement of the tires on the asphalt. I can't help but watch on, transfixed inside of my own private prison, stuck on the roof with no available way to catch a horse.

Giselle saunters by across the quad sidewalk and I recognize her by her orange hair and deliberate movements. In a state of total bewilderment I recognize that she's not even giving heed to the fact that there's a horse standing in the road. I can almost understand Dillon being so preoccupied with his own goings-on that he wouldn't notice the large creature, but Giselle is a woman of observation and introversion, always watching the world around her. This is what makes her good at photography. This is what makes me think that she should notice a horse in the road.

I can almost see the Shad Bay lighthouse from the top of the roof, the peak of the tower bobbing over top of the farthest away trees in a sullen red. There's an unreasonable amount of dichotomy in Riverside - fields, hills, mountains, the ocean - almost as if the place doesn't really exist inside of the realm of the world. But I grip my hands along the edge of the building and the bricks cut into my hands and I know that this is all real.

And there's really a horse in the road.

A truck comes barreling down the street in front of campus, approaching recklessly over the speed limit, and I swear I can hear the bass thumping from the speakers all the way up here in the sky.

Thud, thud, thud.

The percussive banging doesn't startle the horse in the least, though she does stop and stand with her body straddling the centre line, a ribbon of yellow running between her hooves.

Thud, thud, thud.

My heart starts to pound along with the music.
As I watch the driver weave along the curves of the road something becomes abundantly clear: this person doesn't see the horse either.

The mare swishes her tail as the vehicle drives closer, and snorts into the daylight while Giselle opens the door to the sleeping quarters far below me. I had almost forgotten entirely about her existence until I hear the stereotypical slam of the latch over the bass.

Thud, thud, thud.

The truck is twenty feet away. I hold my breath.

Then ten. My lungs constrict.

Then five, four, three, two, one - and I reach out my hand to stifle a scream, knowing the impending nightmare ahead. With my jolted movement I lose my balance and fall.

Time stops.

The world is a blur of greys, browns, and greens around me, the colours slipping together like liquid falling from the sky and melting into an inky, stormy backdrop. My hair sticks to my face and I am blinded by the stinging rain and the howling wind. My ears burn with the sound of the tempest. But my brain, well that, of course, is ignorant of all of the atmosphere and simply drives me forward in a carnal impulse of will and curiosity.

There is a stabbing and curious pain in the left side of my chest, my heart perhaps giving out before the rest of my body impacts the sidewalk.

I have just enough time to watch the horse bleeding to death on the road before I have the wind and the life knocked out of me.

As I impact against the sidewalk I find myself shooting out of bed, Dillon rolls over.

"E? Are you okay?"

I am covered in sweat and my body is red with heat.

"Am I dead?"

Dillon sighs and runs his hand through his hair as he collapses against the spare pillow.

"You're not dead, Ethan."

"But I swear, I totally just -..." The words come out of my mouth in a frantic predisposition.

"Please. It's six in the morning. Go back to sleep."

But I can't. I'm too lost.

So I get up, glancing at the time on my phone I realize Dillon is right - it's only a few hours after we both passed out, lethargic in our mutual high alongside the rising lemonade sky and flossy clouds. The morning is vast and unyielding, as all mornings are, opening the world up to another collection of possibilities in any one of an innumerable amount of random intervals. Birds play along the field lines, drifting up toward Eisan, and the storminess of the day before is washing away and blowing out to the ocean. It looks like the beginning of yesterday, before all the mammatus clouds rolled in.

My clothes are wrinkled and have absorbed all the scents of the room.

Out of habit rather than necessity, I listen at my door before I open it, hoping to avoid Lacey and her minions if any of them happen to be out and about.

There is thankful silence.

The hallway is deserted when I look down toward the washroom corridors. A quiet turning of a handle slips into my ear, and Kelsey's door opens.

"Ethan," Lacey nods toward me, a sheepish look painted on her face.

"What are you doing in Kelsey's room?"

If she notices I'm wearing the same clothes from yesterday she doesn't acknowledge it.

"It's hard to explain." The words come stammering out of Lacey's mouth as she searches for just the right ones.

I stare. That's the only description I have for the face that I'm making - a poignant stare that waits for a better answer.

"It's like this."

She punches me square in the face and I hit the floor like a rock.

The day I arrived at Riverside Academy there was a thunderstorm. The biggest one in the state in the last fifty years, according to the radio of my beat up old Kia Rio. It lasted for almost a full day and into the night - tornado watches and all of that - the blackness only enhancing the sharp glow of the electricity coursing through the air.

I had never seen anything like it, and it was magnificent.

I must get to the cottage, it tells me.

On time with my progress, lightning sears through the sky and slices the scene in front of me; a white-hot lace of fingerling tendrils. The sound temporarily deafens me, closing my eardrums to the pulse throbbing in my veins, and one of the tall, dark shadows ahead crackles and pops and then creaks into the emptiness. I hold my breath for a second, muscles tensing, then I hear the noise I already knew was coming.

It happens slowly, then all at once. The splintering sound of wood separating, the hollow rustle of vacant branches, the air rushing through the emptiness. I duck behind a wooden fence for cover, even though I know the enormity of the tree would crush us both if it fell at the wrong angle. Every dream it falls the same way and every dream I'm safe behind the fence line.

Except this dream. This dream it smashes into my skull with a sickening crunch and I am crushed. My bones collapse in on my organs and I see black.

Dillon isn't there when I jolt awake. Glancing at the time on my phone I realize it's only a few hours after we both passed out - lethargic in our mutual high alongside the rising lemonade sky and flossy clouds. The morning is vast and unyielding, as all mornings are, opening the world up to another collection of possibilities in any one of an innumerable amount of random intervals. Birds play along the field lines, drifting up toward Eisan, and the storminess of the day before is washing away and blowing out to the ocean. It looks like the beginning of yesterday, before all the mammatus clouds rolled in.

The spot next to me in the bed hasn't retained any of Dillon's warmth. It's as if he was never there at all. But I know he must have been there at some point, the spare pillow missed up into the corner of the bedside and the sheets crinkled in a ghostly body shape.

My clothes are wrinkled and have absorbed all the scents of the room.

Out of habit rather than necessity, I listen at my door before I open it, hoping to avoid Lacey and her minions if any of them happen to be out and about.

There is thankful silence.

The hallway is deserted when I look down toward the washroom corridors. A quiet turning of a handle slips into my ear, and Kelsey's door opens.

"Ethan," Mr. Leighton nods toward me, a sheepish look painted on his face.

"What are you doing in Kelsey's room?"

If he notices I'm wearing the same clothes from class yesterday he doesn't acknowledge it.

"It's hard to explain." The words come stammering out of Elliott's mouth as he searches for just the right ones.

I stare. That's the only description I have for the face that I'm making - a poignant stare that waits for a better answer.

"It's like this."

He opens his hand and presents to me a white, glass horse. It's identical in every way to the black horse on my nightstand but the eyes look more hollow - like this horse never came to life.

"Kelsey and I had a special relationship, Ethan. I could never admit it to anyone but I think I can admit it to you."

I bite the inside of my cheek.

"It's perfectly explainable. Kelsey was a brilliant student in some ways but so naive in others. She used to visit my place on weekends and we'd put together these brilliant photoshoots. She'd pose for me and then we would sit on my patio and watch the cars pass by and do lines of coke. It was a beautiful tessellation. A perfect network of our brains creating together."

"I don't get it. You and Kelsey?"

Elliott smiles and I switch uncomfortably from foot to foot.

"Clever girl."

"Where is Kelsey now?" The question fits awkwardly in the conversation but, despite this, Elliott doesn't react as if he's concerned about it.

But he does know something.

"I've just told you that your best friend was a cocaine addict and you're choosing to ignore this fact?"

"Willful blindness, Mr. Leighton." I roll the white horse over in my hands, the mother of pearl finish making tiny rainbows with each movement.

"How can you be willfully blind to your own indiscretions?" He asks the question so simply, leaning against Kelsey's doorframe as if we are the only two people in the entire world.

It's quiet. Eerily quiet.

"What do you mean?"

"Ethan, everyone knows. Just nobody talks about it."

"They do?"

Elliott nods, placing his hands on my shoulders.

"You really need to pull yourself together."

I try to understand him, but I feel as if I'm being sucked into a vortex. The world swirls around me, a tapestry of colour, and for a minute I'm sure I'm going to faint. I drop the white glass horse on the hallway floor and in one swift movement, Elliott smashes it with the heel of his shoe. Tiny ringlets of sparkling smoke twist and twirl around the ashes of the chess piece until it is no more than sand. I look down at the floor, dismayed, and Elliott drops his arms to his sides.

"There is no horse." The words are mumbled but clear enough that I'm certain of their dictation.

"How did you know I saw a horse?" My expression is a mixture of confusion and delirium - at least I think it is.

"You've been talking about a horse for the last ten minutes."

"But I just came out of my room a second ago."

Elliott sighs.

"Come to the roof with me. I'll show you what I'm talking about."

I'm perturbed. But I go with him.

Elliott saunters off down the hall and seemingly expects me to follow him. I suppose I have nothing else to do this early in the morning so I find myself tracking along in his footsteps. Maybe the top of the girls' dorm could have something to do with why I keep seeing the black mare everywhere - just another piece of an uncertain illusion that is taped together over this entire town.

The door upstairs is in the middle of the hallway along the far wall, indicated in a clashing mauvey-rose facade. Usually the entryway and that section of stairwell are kept locked, but to my own benefit Elliott seems to have acquired the key to unlock the doorway and with a bit of jiggling and a couple of curse words, we are able to ascend.

Light shines through the window at the top of the steps. The corridor was dark the last time I remember going up, but I couldn't tell you how long ago that was. Minutes, hours, days - maybe.

The door to the roof opens with a whine, interjecting dissatisfaction on Elliott's plan to stand out in the world. Beams of sun shine brightly on my skin, and Elliott props the door open with a discarded brick to allow ourselves back inside. He motions for me to come out and I hesitate.

"Come, Ethan."

My legs move all of their own volition.

The tips of my fingers and my toes start to tingle, but the sensation doesn't last as long as the first time. I'm not scared of being up so high, per se, but the flatness of the roof combined with the starkness of the distant fields creates a mind game of a flat plain that continues on. I could almost swear it did continue forever - like I could step off the roof and onto the next. But I know to stay away from the edge.

"Lovely start to the weekend." Elliott walks along the crunching stone on the roof, the wind carrying away the details of his words.

Is this Saturday again? Didn't I just have Saturday?

Cars crawl past in a typical Saturday fashion, a little busier than most weekends but definitely with the right flow for Elliott's observation. Riverside isn't exactly a bustling metropolis - but Kia Rios and Honda Civics and other vehicles I can't possibly name make their way through campus. Destination unknown.

I peer shakily down at the campus, light refracting off glossy surfaces, and think about the moment when Elliott is going to ask me about my Faces Magazine submission. The wait is short-lived, unlike my anxiety.

"About your project," Elliott begins. "Tessellation. It's a tough one, isn't it?"

I nod, noticing Dillon's car pulling out of the parking lot.

"The interconnected network of it all. These ties that bind."

Time passes, as it does.

Then I see Kelsey. She's in the middle of the road.

The black of Kelsey's hair glistens with the early sunlight, a midnight canvas against a backdrop of emerald, sand, and bits of mahogany tree bark. She tosses her ponytail in an elegant and refined fashion as she struts down the yellow double line. Traffic has dissipated around the girl, weaving appropriately to avoid her existence, and she appears unaffected by the noise of the road or the movement of the tires on the asphalt. I can't help but watch on, transfixed inside of my own private prison, stuck on the roof with Elliott.

"She's going to get hit." I can feel myself start to panic, recalling how this scenario ended for the black horse.

Elliott is holding a syringe.

"Nobody's in the road, Ethan. You're just coming down. I've got you."

He slips the needle into my arm and I'm too stunned to move. It takes a bit of time for the drugs to sink it but once they do, there is a quiet tranquility that washes over me.

I can almost see the Shad Bay lighthouse from the top of the roof, the peak of the tower bobbing over top of the farthest away trees in a sullen red. There's an unreasonable amount of dichotomy in Riverside - fields, hills, mountains, the ocean - almost as if the place doesn't really exist inside of the realm of the world. It all starts to blend together when I realize Elliott's stuck another needle in my arm.

"Lovely place to die, isn't it, Kelsey?"

I want to correct him and remind him I'm Ethan, but my legs stop working and I collapse onto the gravelly substrate.

Time stops and my pulse slows into a gelatinous lub.

The world is a blur of greys, browns, and greens around me, the colours slipping together like liquid falling from the sky and melting into an inky, stormy backdrop. My hair sticks to my face and I realize I am sweltering here on top of the dormitories. Rocks burn my skin with sounds of a tempest. But my brain, well that, of course, projects for me both a black horse and a white horse standing to my side.

They aren't helping.

All I can hear is sunshine and birds. I feel warm - a creeping, spidery heat.

"You look perfect."

His voice is far away. I muster up as much strength as I possibly can and try to move, my muscles screaming. My body ignores me, shifting a little too much to the left, and then there's air all around me.

Elliott's voice calls a goodbye that trickles down the wind.

I am slammed into concrete, but my bones remain intact.

The woozy, watery feeling remains a constant companion, drowning between my ears in a lethargic worry. A dissipating pinch retracts out of my left arm and the black horse stares at me. She's smaller now, poised on the precipice of a shelf, a wall to the side of me climbing with their simplicity.

I am in a room. But not a room I recognize. And I feel the panic starting to set in.

Turning my head, I come in contact with the rounded bones of a knee.

"Don't move."

The voice is familiar, but my mind cannot process it, the receipt paper of my brain empty and unable to print or authorize any logical conclusion. I can only determine I must have a brain injury, my descent from the top of the sleeping quarters not high enough to kill me, but a great enough distance that I've ended up in the hospital.

But then why am I on the floor?

Did I fall out of the bed?

I take an inventory of myself in an attempt to calm down. My fingers and toes are still numb, the same as they were on top of the roof, the prickling feeling extending past my knuckles and into my hands. I don't think I could move even if I really wanted to. I don't want to. I'm going to die on this floor and everything will be alright.

Hands reach under my arms and lift with curious agility - a man, his body, pressing against my side as my vision starts to clear. Black hair runs down over my shoulders and tangles in his fingers, a cascade of ebony, matching the starless obsidian of the horse on the shelf. As I am hoisted, I can see a collection of other figurines gathered around the horse, and a checkered board on the table below, empty save for one ivory horse. A knight piece.

The overhead light buzzes as I am placed on a soft surface.

"Kelsey?"

I take my best guess at whoever is speaking to me, despite the fact that they're calling me by the wrong name.

"Elliott?" He was the last person I saw so the first to come to mind.

There is laughter.

"You think I'm your father?"

Hair is brushed from my face and I open my eyes to see Dillon, clear as day.

"No," I start explaining to him as if he's a child. "Elliott is Mr. Leighton. You have his class." I sigh, the words jumbling together.

"His first name was Ethan, Kelsey. Elliott is your dad's name."

Oh.

Dillon looks different than I remember in my previous visions. He's still strong and taut but he has haunted eyes and thinning hair that he's buzzed into some kind of military cut. There's a cigarette behind one ear but he's dressed to the nines, khakis skirting along the painted concrete floor. A few rugs break up some of the cold space, but not the solidarity of the room. I know it's minimalist, spatteringly decorated with rich authenticities, but I can only think about how my heart is racing and where Dillon might have taken me.

"Where am I?"

Dillon laughs again, more of a nervous sound than an actual chuckle, and I swear I can see the sound, squiggled lines making their way across the space and hammering into the wall below the black horse. Waves of noise in multi-colours wash their way along the air, blown around by a ceiling fan into a muddled tornado. I sit up against the headboard, the sheets and comforter mussed up under my legs.

"You're in the basement, Kelsey. You've been living here for three years."

I spot the capped needle in his breast pocket.

"What -..."

A sigh from Dillon.

"I'm a doctor, Kelsey. Please."

I am utterly confused, and in my state of unsettled frustration, I begin to ramble.

"You're a macro photographer - I remember you from Riverside. We used to get high and screw around together."

Dillon sits on the edge of the bed and scratches at the back of his neck.

"That was once, first year, Kel. That was a long time ago."

There is a pregnant pause.

I wait for my vision to clear up and give my head a few shakes. I can see the crystal blue of his eyes now, just as I can remember them that night on my futon in the dark. Pieces of my life vacuum their way back into my consciousness, slowly, full of dust and debris.

"What happened to me?" The words are quiet, barely making their way past my parched lips. Dillon gives me a look that is mixed with pity.

"You fell off the roof in first year, Kel. You were high. You thought you saw a horse get hit by a car in the middle of the street."

The pools of blood snake their way back into my memory, crimson and thick with plasma, spreading along the double yellow line. I remember seeing the horse, the black mare, and I remember the vehicle with too much bass crashing into her figure as if it were only yesterday. My memories drop back slowly - by Dillon's estimation, this was almost ten years ago now; many yesterdays ago.

A clock ticks along the farthest away wall and the repetitive noises rap on my brain with the consistency of a hammer.

"Dillon, why am I in your basement?"

He pales, opens his pocket to check the syringe, and places a hand on my leg.

"We're married, Kelsey. We got married in second year. After you fell off the roof."

This sounds odd to me, like it doesn't fit. A piece of a puzzle that's leftover with nowhere to go.

"My name is Ethan."

There is a perfect space of silence for Dillon to sigh again but he doesn't. Instead he fetches another syringe from his pocket. This one is filled with liquid.

My skin pinches and I can feel the solution drip into my body. My eyes get heavy quickly.

"I love you, Kelsey."

Things get hazy.

My eyes close and I drift away.

A second later I'm walking up a forest path in the midst of a thunderstorm, wind whipping around my arms, scratching at the spots my forlorn jacket would normally bandage. The infinitesimal rain barges against the soaking fabric of my clothes, pounding into my jeans, my socks, my shoes, squelching in the grass and the mud and under my toes. My camera hangs around my neck, waiting - ever waiting - for a photograph of a horse to bring me back to life.

Nicole Bea

@nicbeawrites

Cold War

Dinner is the same every night. Juanita prepares dinner to be served by 8:00 p.m., just as Roger likes it. I hand him his scotch when he walks in and ask, "Roger, dear, how was your day?" And he replies, "Fine darling, just fine."

Roger works at Stanford University on very important government projects. He never talks much about it, patting my hand and telling me how boring it is and that I'd never understand what he does. He teases me that if he told me about his work, he'd have to kill me so I couldn't tell some Russian spy his secrets.

He is so considerate of my feelings and has been since the day we met. I was working as a temp at Stanford and he was doing his important work when I accidentally spilled my coffee. I was trying to get coffee, file papers, and answer the telephone for Mr. Frankfeld. Roger was at my desk for his meeting with Mr. Frankfeld. He gave me his handkerchief and saved the files from getting wet. Roger even defended me when Mr. Frankfeld said he'd have me transferred to the psychology department in the basement of the building.

We had two children, now grown up and moved far away. Billy followed his father's footsteps at MIT, and Janie left college when her Tommy returned home from the war. Oh, I get letters every now and then because it is so expensive to make long distance phone calls. It's been quiet around our house since they left. And lonely.

While Roger finishes his drink and we wait for dinner to be served, I tell him about my day since he says the same thing about his day – "Fine dear". I begin my day, same as the day before and the day before that. Juanita arrives around 9:00 a.m., and we review the household chores for the day: laundry, dusting, vacuuming, meal planning, and then the extras if we are entertaining. Juanita came with good references, but heavens to Betsy, I have to watch her constantly. I tell Roger the news from the afternoon bridge game or tennis game or salon appointment while he has his coffee, dessert, and cigarettes. Last week, poor Francine Everton had to dismiss her housekeeper Gloriana. She found that woman in the pool house with Ricardo the gardener. Francine's husband, Arthur, refused to dismiss Ricardo because he is an excellent gardener – best lawn in the neighborhood. Then Francine showed us her expensive pearl necklace Arthur bought her to convince her to accept Ricardo's apology.

By the time I finish about my day, Roger is heading to bed—alone. I didn't tell him about the lovely hat pin given to me by Mr. O'Brien, our milkman; he looks just like Gary Cooper, the movie star. He took over the route from Old Mr. Haverton and is very attentive. He stops by quite often to check on us and make sure his deliveries are what I ordered. Sometimes we have coffee, with cream of course, and talk about how busy Roger is these days, and how his job is so important – I certainly wouldn't want him to lose it.

Tonight's dinner is unusual. Roger arrived home early. His drink is not ready, so he helped himself. He tells Juanita she could leave early, and that I would serve the dinner. I am tired from a long day of shopping, but he is in a mood, so I didn't say anything. He was on his second scotch and already smoking a cigarette, staring out the front window at the unruly neighbor children jumping rope in the driveway across the street. Don't they know that dinner is a time for quiet? I call him to dinner. He kisses me on the cheek as usual and sits down. I fix his plate, then my own. I try to be cheerful, thinking of some clever story I could tell him about my day at the department store.

"How was your day, Roger, dear?" I automatically ask, cutting into my meatloaf, thinking of the silly clerk who thought I wore a size 9 wide shoe.

These young women really need more training before they are allowed on the sales floor. I'll have to talk to the manager next time I am there.

"Today, I finalized the blueprints for a missile that could reach Russia," he said slowly, spooning more gravy over his mashed potatoes, "or the house of that milkman who lives five blocks from here."

He looks at this watch and then at the front door and finishes his scotch.

I stare at him, my fork automatically lifting the peas and carrots to my open mouth. The doorbell rings, and Roger lets in two men in dark suits. I hear the tinkle of glass on the front porch as they knock over the empty milk bottles waiting for Mr. O'Brien. Still sitting at the table with my napkin in my lap, Roger nods at me, and they walk calmly toward me, not saying a word. Juanita will have more than the dishes to clean up when she comes in tomorrow.

"Could we use the back door so the neighbors won't see? They really need to mind their own business," I plead as the men each take my arm and begin to escort me to the front door. I manage to grab my hat and bag, even though my hands are shaking.

"Roger? Your shirts will be ready tomorrow after three. The ticket is on your bureau," I shout. "Don't forget! They will charge us more if you forget!" The men force me out the back door of my own home. Over my shoulder, I see Roger in the doorway, twirling the hat pin between his fingers.

Susan Sinclair Edele

Follow us on social media for news,
updates, and our full catalog
of fiction and nonfiction.

Purchase the latest issue of our magazine
by visiting our website.

facebook.com/DarkInkPress
@DarkInk_Press
@DarkInkPress